Return to Lesbos

FEMMES FATALES

Femmes Fatales restores to print the best of women's writing
in the classic pulp genres of the mid-twentieth century. From mysteries
to hard-boiled noir to taboo lesbian romance, these rediscovered
queens of pulp offer subversive perspectives on a turbulent era.

Faith Baldwin
SKYSCRAPER

Vera Caspary
BEDELIA
LAURA
THE MAN WHO LOVED HIS WIFE

Gypsy Rose Lee
THE G-STRING MURDERS
MOTHER FINDS A BODY

Evelyn Piper
BUNNY LAKE IS MISSING

Olive Higgins Prouty
NOW, VOYAGER

Valerie Taylor
THE GIRLS IN 3-B
STRANGER ON LESBOS
RETURN TO LESBOS

Tereska Torrès
WOMEN'S BARRACKS
BY CECILE

Return to Lesbos

VALERIE TAYLOR

THE FEMINIST PRESS
AT THE CITY UNIVERSITY OF NEW YORK
NEW YORK CITY

Published in 2013 by the Feminist Press
at the City University of New York
The Graduate Center
365 Fifth Avenue, Suite 5406
New York, NY 10016

feministpress.org

First Feminist Press edition

Cover and text design by Drew Stevens.

Library of Congress Cataloging-in-Publication Data
Taylor, Valerie, 1913–1997
 Return to Lesbos / Valerie Taylor.
     pages cm
 "Originally published by Tower Publications in 1963."
 ISBN 978-1-55861-832-9
1. Lesbians—Fiction. 2. Jewish gays—Fiction.
3. Holocaust survivors—Fiction. I. Title.
PS3570.A957R4 2013
813'.54—dc23
                                    2013017571

1

KARLA'S PLACE WAS JUMPING. FRANCES OLLENFIELD stood at the edge of the sidewalk and watched the blue door swinging open and shut behind the couples: two girls in bermudas and knee socks, two slim boys moving gracefully in unison, more girls. Smoke and voices and juke music drifted out. Frances shivered a little, although it was a June evening in Chicago.

She hadn't been in a gay bar for a year. She had promised never to visit one again. But her need was too strong. She took a deep breath and walked down the three stone steps, feeling her mouth go dry and her heart begin to hammer with excitement. The blue paint was flaking off the door and the gold scroll letters had faded. It's been a while, Frances thought.

Inside, though, nothing had changed. The Friday-night crowd was out: all the tables were taken and there wasn't an empty stool at the bar. The space around the jukebox was jammed with slowly moving dancers, boys with boys and girls with girls. The faces were different, but the crowd was the same.

Past a row of heads and shoulders she could see Mickey at the bar, rosy cheeked and as happy looking as ever, her curly dark hair combed flat and her Ivy League shirtsleeves rolled up. Frances felt better. Mickey never forgot a customer. Seeing a couple pocket their change and get up, she elbowed a path across the crowded room and took one of the vacated stools. She said in a low voice, "Hi, Mickey."

1

"Well, hi. Martini?"

"That's right."

"You haven't been around for a while," Mickey said, swabbing a section of counter with a pink cellulose sponge. "You went back to your husband, didn't you?"

She looked sharply at Mickey. Mickey met the look straight on. "I didn't mean to be nosy, only you used to come in with that Baker chick all the time. I see her once in a while."

With her new girl, Frances thought bitterly. She said, "Yeah, I went back to my husband. It hasn't worked out very well."

"Never does," Mickey assured her cheerfully. She set the drink down and bustled off to the other end of the bar. Frances sat holding the cold glass in her hand, looking around hungrily. She had been away too long.

At the next table sat two girls who might possibly have been twenty-one, as the state liquor laws required, but she doubted it. One was small and delicate looking, with long fair hair hanging thick to her waist, the way only a hip type would wear it in a year of tortured and teased bouffant styles. The other, older, had a sharp knife-blade profile, Turkish or possibly Indian. They weren't touching one another, but appeared to be set apart in a little capsule of time and space, existing only for each other. Here, at least, they could look their love and not be afraid of what outsiders would think. Frances's eyes stung with envy and pity. They were so young—and so lucky—and so much sorrow still lay ahead of them.

Bake wasn't there, or Jane. She was both disappointed and relieved.

The door opened and shut behind a new couple, a tall thin girl in the standard getup of tapered slacks, knit shirt, and loafers, her friend a slight redhead like the young Edna Millay. Behind them, alone, stood a third who was familiar to her even through the eddies of smoke and the shifting figures passing and re-passing. Kay.

She stood still for a moment, lighting a cigarette, sizing up the place as she always did, indifferent to what other people thought of her. Feeling she had to talk to her, Frances started to slip down from the bar stool. But at that moment Kay caught sight of her, signaled a greeting with lovely dark eyebrows and made her unhurried way across the room. People moved to let her pass. Her hands were warm and light on Frances's shoulders. She said, "Hello, darling!"

"Hi."

"Bring your drink to a table." Kay caught Mickey's eye. Mickey came over with a smile of real welcome. "Those fellows are about ready to leave," she said happily. "Martini for you too?"

"Right."

They settled down, beaming at each other.

"Kay, tell me everything."

"Well, Bake and Jane are still together. Your girl and my girl; it looks like it's lasting." Kay unbuttoned the jacket of her office suit and relaxed against the back of the chair. "Jane looks fine. They both do. Naturally I hate to admit it." She grinned. "Bake's more or less on the wagon, and they're talking about buying a place in the suburbs."

Frances went silent. Three years with Bake, then the stormy breaking-up; had it all simmered down to this? Her throat hurt. She picked up her glass, seeing her hand tremble.

Kay went on talking. "I'm in the midst of packing. Got a government job in Iran. I've been cleared by security and everything, it's lucky we don't have as much trouble as the boys—if a boy looks the least bit swishy he's had it, even if they can't prove anything."

"You're going alone?"

"Sure. Maybe I'll find somebody over there." Kay accepted a glass from Mickey and gave her a dollar bill and a warm smile. "Losing Jane hit me pretty hard. I've played around a little, but it wasn't the same. So I decided it was time for a change of scenery."

"Sounds exciting."

"So what's with you? I suppose you're not 100 percent happy or you wouldn't be here. Or are you slumming?"

"I've done my best," Frances said. She was thinking out

3

loud; the bitterness in her voice came as a surprise to her. "You know, my husband took me back the day our son got married. He was so noble and so forgiving—Christ, I've gone on being forgiven for a whole year now, and I can't take much more of it! I don't think he realizes yet, but it can't go on. I've worked like hell for a year—"

"And what have you got to show for it?"

"A whole lot of nothing."

Now it was in words. She had not been able to admit it before, even to herself, but Kay's eyes demanded honesty. She said again, confused but insistent, "I did try."

"And how's your son?"

"Fine. It's his first wedding anniversary today. He's still in college—just finishing his freshman year." Frances hesitated. "They're going to have a baby in the late winter. I hate to think about it."

"Oh well, you married young. You're a good-looking girl, Francie."

Frances shrugged. "It does me a lot of good."

"No fun in bed? With Bill, I mean?"

"It's the same old rabbit routine. He's finished before I start to get warmed up."

"And you haven't looked for anybody else?"

"Honest I haven't." This was serious. It was important that Kay know she had done her best—if it hadn't worked out, someone else was to blame. She shook her head to clear it. "I've truly tried."

"I'm sure of it." Kay's voice was gentle. "The trouble is, Francie, you're gay. What you had with Bake wasn't just a bored housewife having a fling—I know that's what your husband thinks. It was the real thing. You belong on our side of the fence, 100 percent."

"I know it now."

"I married a man too, you know. It's true my husband was a son-of-a-bitch, but that has nothing to do with the fact that I've never wanted another man." She looked hard at Frances. "I honestly don't think an unhappy marriage ever made a lesbian out of any girl. It just brings out what's already there."

"You left your husband to be with Jane, didn't you?"

"Yes, and I've never been sorry. It was worth it."

Frances sighed. "Maybe you're smarter than I am. I thought I could make a go of marriage."

"Maybe you could if you'd thrown away your whole personality, everything you are and could be. I think that's evil." Kay reached across the table and touched her hand. "So what happens next?"

Frances's smile was strained. "So now Bill's being transferred out to the boondocks, and I'm supposed to go along and be a good little company wife. He'd be shocked to death if I told him I didn't want to go."

"Are you going?"

"How can I help it?"

"Sooner or later you'll have to face up to it. You'll meet a girl you want. It always happens. The only thing that surprises me is, it hasn't happened already. Then how are you going to break the news to him?"

Frances said unbelievingly, "In Waubonsie, Illinois?"

"Anywhere you go," Kay said patiently, setting down her drink, "you'll find members of the club. Carefully disguised of course, you have to be discreet in a small place, you can't keep your business and personal life separated the way you do in a big city. But you'll find somebody you want to have an affair with. Believe me."

"Will you? In Iran?"

"If I don't, I'm coming back the minute my contract's up." Kay grinned. "Arab men are famous for it. That must leave the women with a lot of free time on their hands."

Frances said in a low voice, "My contract's for life."

"That's not a contract, that's a prison sentence." Kay raised her eyebrows. "Moving isn't going to make a goddamn bit of difference. Gay in a straight world and hip in a square one. We ought to be glad we're white, that's one problem we don't have anyhow."

Tears came into Frances's eyes and spilled warm and wet

down her cheeks. She gave a little quavering sigh like a child's. "Kay, I'm so miserable. I don't know what to do."

"Make up your mind," Kay said. She beckoned to Mickey, who was waiting with two more drinks. "The thing is to decide what you are and then learn to live with yourself. Don't try to make yourself over. There's no percentage in it."

Frances stared at her glass. She said resentfully, "You make it sound so simple."

"It's the truth. And I promise you," Kay said, smiling a little, "if you really want someone to love, you'll find someone. Never fails. That's a promise."

2 FRANCES WAS STILL CLUTCHING AT THAT PROMISE two weeks later, when she and Bill moved.

It was raining in Waubonsie. Mood weather, Frances thought, sitting upright beside Bill with her hands folded on her lap, looking like a housewife with nothing on her mind but packing cases. Or so she hoped. Maybe it always rained in Waubonsie—like Liverpool.

"Still worried about your dishes?"

"Why not?" She didn't give a damn if every plate she owned got broken in transit. Life ought to be something more than dishes. You could always buy new ones—it was one way to pass the time.

"Tired?"

"Kind of."

Suspiciously, "You're not going to get temperamental, are you?"

Frances said sharply, "Not unless it's temperamental to have your back ache from packing."

"I told you to get a professional mover. You don't have to put on the big martyr act."

"I didn't have anything else to do."

She *had* been acting like a martyr. Might as well admit it. As though to punish herself for her perfidious thoughts by working extra hard. I will be a good wife, she resolved for the umpteenth time, looking out of the rain-drenched window. They were driving past a wood-working plant: soaked window frames stacked against the side of a low brick building, a pile of scrap lumber overflowing onto the sidewalk. Men stripped to the waist, their wet work pants molded to their legs, were loading backed-up trucks. Frances felt a qualm of envy as they disappeared from view. Silly, she thought, they're no more free than you are, they probably all have wives and kids at home; they're probably all making payments on those ugly little crackerbox houses and a lot of washers and dryers. But she envied them for a moment, working in the rain.

What waited for her at the end of the ride was even worse than she had pictured.

"Maybe you're not going to be so crazy about the house," Bill said, rounding a corner and peering through the rain at the street sign. "I guess you like modern architecture—well, some day we can afford to build, maybe. I told Bowers we'd sublease his place for a year; he's made a big down payment and he stands to lose everything if he can't find a tenant." He sounded angry. It wasn't in the picture of the successful American executive to be sick and harassed by money worries. "The damn fool won't ever be able to do a full day's work again; I might as well figure the job's mine for keeps. Time we settled down and made ourselves part of some community, anyhow."

She didn't say anything.

"Anyway, there's a nice big yard," Bill continued. "It's a good neighborhood, too."

Frances cleared a segment of windshield with her hand and tried not to be nervous as he eased the car into a driveway between two square houses with bay windows. She said, "I'll have to buy an aspidistra."

"Huh?"

The house was large and solid, set firmly in the middle of a lawn with several trees in front and some non-blooming plants along the side walls. The first story had been painted white, but not recently, and the second story was bright yellow under a roof of wavy tan and brown asbestos shingles. Like a layer cake with fudge icing, Frances thought. She had sense enough not to say so.

A wide, railed porch ran across the front of the house. A concrete walk led to the front steps and another, narrower strip of concrete led around the house, to a side door where a green plastic hose dangled snakelike from a faucet. Oh goody, I can spend the long summer evenings watering the lawn.

Bill said, "This is it. Might as well go in."

She got out of the car gingerly, holding her storm coat around her, trying not to step on the rubbery, pink angleworms spread on the grayish walk. Not exactly a tropical paradise, and who's going to mow all this grass? She started bravely for the front door, trying not to feel that every step brought her closer to the prison gates.

The door stood open. Beyond the cavernous hall, lights bloomed. As they stood hesitant—Bill not quite sure, she thought, that this was the right house—women spilled out to meet them. Only five women, but making enough noise and shedding enough goodwill for twenty. The Young Married ones, thirtyish, in capri pants that showed their backyard tans. Frances stood dripping in her old trench coat, which was overdue at the cleaner's, while they came burbling up and told her their names. Rose Sanderson, wife of the credit manager at the plant. Tisi Murphy, whose husband was head of the shipping room. Betsy Chancellor, wife of the purchasing agent. And so on. She wondered, didn't they have anything to do but be wives? She should have expected something like this. Stupid not to. The miners' wives back home used to do it too—social customs apparently were the same everywhere, whether you were a plant manager's wife in tight pink pants or the wife of a mine foreman. She didn't quite know how to react. Her parents had lived on the other side of the tracks—in a company town the criteria are piety and cleanliness rather than managerial status, but the principle is the same.

It was different here. Her husband was boss over all these women's husbands, he made more than they did—and, too, her figure was better than any of theirs. For a moment she shared and understood the concern of women for position, a leaky umbrella in a rainy world.

She said, "I look terrible." They were around her, hemming her in, assuring her that she looked fine and hadn't they been through it all? The redhead in pink pants said vehemently, "Moving is hell, isn't it? There's coffee in the kitchen, and Jo-Jo brought cups. Paper makes it taste horrible."

"Besides, we have to use all the plastic we can."

They're so friendly, Frances thought, warmed against her will by this show of neighborliness. She followed them into the house, looking into the rooms they passed but getting only an impression of bareness. The kitchen was bare too, but new linoleum and a shining, huge refrigerator brightened it and the overhead light was on. Someone had spread paper on the work counter, and an electric percolator was glugging. The redhead said, "We had the gas and electricity turned on, but you can't get a telephone before next week. Feel free to use ours—we're two doors over."

How friendly would they be if they knew what I used to be? What I still am.

They wouldn't throw stones at me. Probably wouldn't even be rude to my face. Just snicker behind my back, and feel sorry for Bill.

She said, "I haven't had a chance to look the house over yet, but I know our furniture's going to rattle around in it."

A freckle-faced blonde said, "We have some good stores here. Interior decorators, too. Besides, it's only sixty miles to Chicago, and the big stores ship everything out by truck, so you only have to wait one day. Most of us get into Chicago every few weeks, do a little shopping and see a show. My bridge club and painting class both go once in a while."

Frances took the cup somebody offered her. It was nice and warm in her cold fingers; she shifted it from hand to hand to get the full benefit.

"This would be a good house to do in Victorian. There's even a bay window in the dining room. Victorian's very good now."

Sure. Dark wood, marble-topped tables and funereal footstools in fringed and tasseled velvet. Frances said a little shrilly, "I'm afraid I like contemporary," and let it lie there. Someone tactfully switched the talk to the new plant—or maybe it wasn't tact, the conversation kept coming back to plastics—and there was a respectful little huddle around Bill.

Frances stood drinking coffee, leaning against the doorjamb. Some of the furniture was still on the way and the rest sat huddled in the wrong rooms, looking shabbier than she remembered it. She felt that she could use a drink. There would be drinks at parties, she knew, unless one of the top men was ultra-religious, but apparently protocol didn't permit it at picnics, even indoor picnics. But at least they hadn't brought over a lot of potato salad.

The redhead was saying, "You're probably in a hurry to get settled, but we'd love to have you spend the night at our place. I mean, feel free to say yes or no."

"Thanks," Bill said, managing not to meet his wife's eyes. "They've got a bed set up and I guess we can find everything we need, but thanks just the same. It's mighty nice of you."

The redhead said, "You'll find this is a nice friendly bunch. We get along pretty well together."

I just bet they do. Morning coffee together every morning, and shopping trips and PTA committees. Probably just walk in without knocking. Maybe a full-time job, something to get me out of the house?

Bill put his arm around her as they stood in the doorway, seeing the guests off. His face was high colored and his eyes slightly bloodshot from the long drive; he needed a shave. He said cheerfully, "That was nice of the girls, wasn't it? They seem like nice kids."

"Sure."

"You didn't act too friendly."

"You know it takes me a while to get acquainted."

"Yeah. The thing you have to remember is, it makes a big difference in a place like this. People aren't cold and impersonal in the way they are in a big city. These gals run around together all the time."

She tried to pull away. "I'm a small-town girl, remember?"

Bill said in a wheedling voice, "Don't be crabby." There was no doubt about what was on his mind. She had seen that look too many times before, the fatuous but determined look of a man set on going to bed with his woman.

He said, pressing against her, "Come on upstairs. You haven't even seen the upstairs yet. There're four bedrooms and a sewing room, or whatever you want to use it for, and the guy Bowers bought it from is supposed to put all new fixtures in the bathroom. You can pick them out."

"That's nice. When it quits raining I'll bring my suitcase up and have a bath. I'm tired out."

"You'll feel better after a good nap. Come on upstairs and lie down for a while."

"Oh, Christ!"

"Don't be that way."

She let herself be led up the stairs, feeling his body solid and urgent against hers. With every intention of being a good wife, even a cooperative wife, she couldn't relax or smile or even look at him. His self-conscious methods embarrassed her. She let him lead her from room to room, a husbandly arm around her waist; she predicted accurately the moment when his hand would creep up and cup her breast. He left the room with the bed till last, of course.

If he only didn't act like sex was something to be ashamed of. There had been some good times early in their marriage, not many, but a few, enough to make her feel that all might not be lost—if he would only leave the light on, and take her as though love were a joy and not an embarrassing necessity, like having to go to the bathroom.

Frances saw no reason why she shouldn't do anything she felt like doing when she was bedded down with someone she loved. And she had tried with Bill, not too long after their reunion. Scared but desperate and determined to salvage what she could for both of them, she had asked him to perform the acts that made her happy. He was so shocked that he sat up in bed. "Where did you find out about such things?" he wanted to know, his voice heavy with suspicion. When she told him of the book she had read, his silence let her know that he thought she was lying. To Bill's way of thinking there was only one way she could have learned about such goings-on, and he wasn't going to discuss it.

She had never brought the matter up again.

I guess that takes care of that, she thought, looking dully at the empty sewing room, the large bathroom, the two completely empty rooms that looked small and shabby as empty rooms do, no matter how recently they have been painted and papered. In the two front bedrooms the familiar beds and dressers were standing at all angles, but at least the beds had been set up and the box springs and mattresses pulled into place. Trust Bill to take care of any details that would make him comfortable.

He left his socks on, like a man in a hurry to get it over with and get back to work. She undressed with shaking hands, trying not to feel like a virgin facing defloration. Shut your eyes, she reminded herself. It's not so bad if you shut your eyes.

He was neither harsh nor tender. It was the same as before, as mechanical as eating or washing dishes. He'd make a wonderful machine operator, she thought, sighing wearily, as he rolled over and lay beside her.

She got up and pulled her clothes on, ignoring him. "What's the hurry?"

"I'm cold."

"Well, I ought to get up and go over to the plant for a while anyhow."

She felt sticky and smeary and she wanted a bath. Instead, she went downstairs, trying to take her mind off what had just happened. Standing beside the dining room window, she looked out on a view almost identical with the one she had left behind on Chicago's South Side: a brick house next door, a wider expanse of lawn and healthier-looking flowers here, a tricycle forgotten in the rain.

She wondered where Kay was at this moment and what she was doing. And Bake. But that hurt, the thought of Bake and Jane having a rainy Saturday at home. She tried to think about

Karla's instead. If I were there I'd pick somebody up. Anybody. Anybody would be better than this.

But Karla's was a million miles away and a million years ago. She had made her choice. The door was shut.

In a few minutes Bill came down, wearing his old jacket and slacks but with his hair neatly combed. "If you don't care I think I'll run over to the shop a few minutes—see how they're making out. We're running a skeleton crew on Saturdays till we go into full production. You don't mind staying alone for a while, do you?"

"Of course not."

He couldn't look at her. Never could after one of these daytime performances. He said, "I'll bring back a pizza or something."

"That'll be nice."

The good provider. He would probably let her have a Victorian sofa bristling with red velvet and brass tacks, if she showed any sign of wanting one. Or a mink stole. Anything, except the right to be herself.

When the sound of the car died away she locked the doors and searched methodically through all the cupboards, hoping insanely that someone had left a bottle. They hadn't, of course. She wandered into the living room and sat down on the sofa (not Victorian, but late Sears Roebuck) and looked out at the dripping rain.

I'm not a good wife, she thought dismally. I'm not even a very good whore. I don't know what I am.

3
FURNISHING AN EIGHT-ROOM HOUSE IS WORK, BUT it comes to an end eventually. Two weeks after that rainy moving day, Frances backed down off a stepladder and stood looking up at her new curtains. There wasn't another thing she could do to the place. Not one.

Now what?

Bill was apparently there to stay. He had given her a guided tour of the place, pointing out the solid foundations, hardwood floors and full-size basement and attic. The bathroom and downstairs lavatory were not only tiled with real tile but equipped with copper piping guaranteed to last a lifetime. The roof was fireproof, the siding waterproof. What more could anybody want?

A home-owner's pride colored his voice when he suggested, "You could make a swell TV room down here. Put in one of those portable bars."

"Why don't you mention it to Mr. Bowers?"

His look accused her of treason. "Hell, he'll never get back to work. He ought to retire and move to Florida or someplace where it's warm. Be glad if I took the place off his hands."

She was trapped, then. These were the prison walls closing in around her, decked out in new large-figure wallpaper.

Standing at the foot of the ladder, she wondered bleakly how Kay's confident prophecy was going to come true. She might take a male lover—what was a little adultery in the executive echelons? But if she made a pass at a girl—wow!

She supposed it happened now and then, in a country where one-tenth of all women were supposed to be gay. But she knew, miserably, that Bill would be suspicious of any friendship she made. His ostentatious forgiveness didn't stretch that far. And it made her miserable to tell lies.

She couldn't discuss it with him. He went all tight lipped and gimlet eyed whenever they passed a butch type on the street. It was no use to argue that "the girls" were like everybody else, except in their sex life—and that wasn't as different as he thought! She couldn't say, "Look, we're people too." He wouldn't let her bring the subject up.

And yet, according to the law of averages, two or three of the chicks in his office had to belong. Secretary, file clerk, ad writer, switchboard operator.

Thinking about it made her restless. She showered, pulled on a printed blue silk dress with a little ruffle at the neck—a Mrs. William Ollenfield dress, chosen to conform to Bill's idea of a womanly woman—and doused herself with Je Reviens. She'd go downtown and look at clothes. Have a facial, manicure, hair-tint job, wave and set—hell, why not have her nose pierced too, while she was at it? She might even eat lunch in a tearoom, something squishy in a patty shell, and a fattening dessert. It was what the Wives would do.

Maybe if you did the housewife bit for ten or fifteen years you got used to it. Maybe a fifteen-minute bedding twice a week, without active participation, came to stand for sex. A pretty prospect.

THE CABBIE SAID, "Where you want to go, lady?"

She gave him her best smile. "I don't know, I'm new in town. Where's the best place to get my hair done?"

He looked her over carefully, twisting around in the seat. Apparently she qualified. "There's Shapiro's. That's about the best store in town, and they got a regular beauty parlor. They got everything Marshall Field's has, except the escalator."

"All right, let's try Shapiro's."

She gave him fifty cents more than the meter said, and he thanked her politely but without enthusiasm and drove away, leaving her standing in a completely strange place, trying to organize her thoughts.

This was Main Street. The sign at the corner said so, and besides it looked like Main Street. Parking meters, stores, banks, traffic lights. Shapiro's was four stories high. The Waubonsie State Savings and Loan towered five floors above it, on the corner. She already felt at home with the Savings and Loan; a book of its pale-green checks lay alongside the lipstick in her handbag.

Shapiro's was air-conditioned. She went in, past the display windows with a few summer evening frocks and accessories, past the lady clerks who were surely older than their hair styles and younger than their feet, past the impulse tables of jewelry and gloves, suntan lotion, and dark glasses. In this familiar setting her timidity melted away. She was wafted to the top floor in a slow elevator piloted by a young tan girl in white gloves, and found the beauty salon by the acrid smell of wave lotion. The reception desk was standard and so was the reception: they were booked solid, but they would try to fit her in.

She chose one of a long row of identical metal mesh chairs and looked around at the other waiting women. They all looked married. Business girls, of course, would come in on their lunch hour. Halfway through her second cigarette the receptionist said, "Miss Bernadette will take you now," and there was Miss Bernadette, plump and pleasant in her yellow nylon uniform. With a wedding ring.

But it seemed to her that surely, if she looked searchingly and didn't miss anybody, she would find someone. Her hair rinsed and dried and baked into little tight curls, she sat through the boredom of a manicure. The woman at the next table, having her nails tinted a pale silvery mauve, was slim, gray haired, haughty. She returned Frances's inquiring look with the polite disinterest of one to whom other women are only relatives or neighbors.

I give up, Frances thought. But she was unable to give up. A need she didn't want to admit sent her through the aisles of the store, looking at the counter displays, buying a box of stationery here and three pairs of sheer nylons there, sizing up the clerks and the women who were desultorily shopping. She knew she was being silly. She and Bake and the others had talked about the wacky idea people have that "you can always tell." The men in the insurance office had bragged about "knowing one every time," looking past her as she sat filling out forms. Every woman in the room could be available and it wouldn't show. "Still," Kay had insisted, "sometimes you sort of know. It's not the clothes or the hairdo. I don't know what it is." And Bake, flicking out her cigarette, "Pure wishful thinking."

Frances kept on looking.

It was a hot day. Her back ached from shoving furniture around and her scalp itched from the wave lotion. Her toes pinched. She went out into the torrid street carrying her packages, remembering too late that she had meant to look at dresses.

There were other stores, none so large or up-to-date as Shapiro's but all carrying familiar brand names. A Sears Roebuck on one corner faced a Steinway on the other corner. Kresge,

Woolworth, and Ben Franklin were lined up on the same block. There were jewelry stores with engagement rings in little slotted boxes. She passed a tavern that looked cool and dark, thought about going in for a pre-luncheon martini and realized that she didn't know the customs in Waubonsie. Maybe nice women didn't go into bars unescorted. She walked along.

What was she looking for, she wondered, an oriental bazaar with teak and spices and carved ivory?

A sign with Chinese characters, red on gold, caught her eye. She moved toward it. And there was her bazaar.

The window was narrow, with a dozen books lying at careless angles. A complete edition of Shakespeare in half calf, open at the Balcony Scene—nice clear print with curly serifs and elegant capitals. Half a dozen remaindered novels. A thin volume that could only be hand-set poetry, jacketed in burlap. Katherine Mansfield's *Journals*, both volumes, faded purple. And in the front of the window, flanked by a chunk of uncut rose crystal and a small, flowered bowl, lay a wood carving of a cat done with love and skill, the essence of catness. I've got to have that, she decided, entering to a thin tinkle of chimes.

A young man floated forward to meet her. If she had felt baffled about the women in the store, unable to tell which were her own kind, there was no doubt about this boy. The insurance salesmen would have placed him without a second look. His face was pretty rather than handsome, his hair a little too long and too carefully disposed; he came to an elegant stop leaning on the counter. It was shirtsleeve weather, but his narrow striped collar was held by a little gold pin. A little fine-drawn, a little precious; and in this alien land her heart warmed to him. She could have hugged him.

A little nellie, she thought in automatic criticism. And realized, reddening, that he was sizing her up too and what he was seeing was Mrs. William Ollenfield. She was a little angry that he should judge by appearances. The boys are all artistic and the girls are all athletic. Kay, for instance—Kay wouldn't walk across the street if she had cab fare. She said coldly, "The cat in the window—it's for sale?"

"It's nice, isn't it? I have a friend who carves them. All different and individual—you'll never see it duplicated."

She was reluctant to ask what it cost, as though originality could be paid for in money. It didn't matter anyway. Mrs. William Ollenfield had plenty for little impulsive purchases. Looking around, delaying her commitment to the cat, she saw that the place was really a secondhand store, a little dusty and shabby. But a length of Persian silk in dull reds and blues lay across a small table, there were three or four small water colors on one wall, and a shelf held several pieces of handmade pottery. "The pictures?"

He made a small modest gesture. "Mine. I have fun doing them, and every once in a while somebody buys one." He smiled. "Why don't you look around, if you're not in any hurry? I mean, if you're interested in books. You don't have to buy anything."

It was true, the place was empty except for the two of them. She knew the story: the boy sensitive, working in a store or an office at a job perhaps made for him by an uncle or friend of the family, always out of things, always nervous about his hidden personal life. Dismissals, the staff being cut, the company reorganized, never the real reason, always an embarrassed excuse.

He was looking at her. She said, "Thanks, maybe I will. I just moved here from Chicago, and I haven't met anybody yet." And remembered the freshly curled hair and the printed silk, the idiotic ruffle. Take off your mask, but how? He said politely, "It's not a very interesting town," and turned away. She had no answer. If she said, "Yes, but I have to go where my husband goes," it would only bear out the lying testimony of the ruffled dress.

It seemed odd, now, that she had never had a close male friend. Bake had half a dozen, two nice boys who shared an apartment on the floor above her, a gray-haired man with an invalid wife who took her to concerts—you saw him in Karla's now and then, having a drink with one girl or another before going back to his furnished room. But she had never known any man well enough to count him as a friend. She thought she might like to know this boy better.

The doorbell jingled again. Sunshine poured in, outlining the figure of a girl on the threshold. She came in slowly, pulling the door shut behind her. In outline, against the harsh outdoor light, she seemed like a slender boy of fifteen or sixteen, his angles not yet blunted into manhood. Once in the room she was neither fifteen nor a boy. There were fine creases at the corners of her eyes and around her thin neck, and the line of her shoulders was purely feminine. She had high cheekbones and ash-blonde hair cut short; where it curled around her forehead it was dark with perspiration. She wore blue slacks and a striped cotton shirt, with sneakers; her bare ankles were fine-boned.

She said, ignoring Frances, "I just wanted to tell you the committee meets tonight at Joe's. The books they ordered have come."

"All right."

I ought to leave, Frances thought. They know each other and I'm an outsider. But she was unable to go. Embarrassed and a little frightened, but compelled, she said, "You look like someone I know."

"Are you a parent? I'm a teacher, so naturally I meet a lot of parents."

"No. I only meant—"

She was floundering. The boy came to her rescue. He said, "She's new in town and she likes John's cats. If she has any sense at all," he said, lifting his narrow shoulders, "she'll go right back where she came from. No matter where it is, it can't be as bad as here."

The girl was sizing her up. Frances gave back the look. She looked like Kay. There was no real physical resemblance; Kay was taller and more filled out, and her hair was reddish-brown. It was the boylike air. Put this one in tights and tunic and she could play Rosalind, half boy and half woman, a face crossed by fleeting part-expressions. Looks or no looks, in some way that really mattered, she was like Kay.

She said, "No, you look like a girl I know. Used to know.

Would you both like to go somewhere and have a drink?"

The appraising silence was like Kay's, too. Then the fair girl gave her a polite smile with no depth to it. "Thanks, but I have an engagement. Maybe another time."

Frances was helpless. She wanted to grab this stranger by the sleeve and beg her not to go away. To say, "Look at me, listen to me, I'm not what you think I am, so don't look at this disguise I have on. I'm your kind of person and I need to know you. Because I've been away from home for a long time."

You can't do these things.

She might be wrong, tricked by an accidental resemblance. She stood silent while the girl left, the little bell over the door fading away into silence. Walking lightly in dirty sneakers, moving like a dancer, she was gone.

The boy said, "Don't let Erika bother you. She's a wonderful person and she's had a rough time. Her best friend was killed in an accident last winter and she was in the hospital for a long time."

"I like her."

The statement fell on its face. He let it lie there. "Why don't you just browse around, if you feel like it, and I'll be in the back room if you find something you like. My name is Vince," he added with a charming smile.

She was too confused to look at books. She bought the carved cat, paid for it and left clutching it, with change in her sweaty hand.

The heat didn't bother her now, or the toe-pinching shoes, or the fact that she had missed both breakfast and lunch. She walked unseeing through the noon streets without considering where she was going. At the corner she almost bumped into a woman who swerved aside to miss her, then called her by name. Half a block later she realized that it was one of the Wives— which one, she had no idea. It didn't matter.

Thank God, there was someone. Someone whose last name she didn't know, who had barely spoken to her and then only to rebuff her. Erika, a teacher—and she had lost someone in a tragic accident. "Best friend" was the way Vince had put it, of course. That meant she was alone and probably lonely.

I have to see her again, Frances thought, worried. But how? And how to undo this horrible first impression?

Through the bookstore boy, of course. Anyone can buy books.

It was after twelve. The sun stood high in the sky behind a stone church with square towers, flying buttresses, and the most lurid stained glass windows she had ever seen, dominating a downtown corner as though the town had grown up around it. As it probably had.

She felt tired. She signalled a cruising cab.

Halfway home, she remembered that she had left her nylons and letter paper in the bookstore. That meant she would have to go back and pick them up. Blessed Freudian slip, giving her a good excuse for what she most wanted to do.

It was Friday, the end of the week. There was the weekend to get through, and a triumphant Bill who was already in the swing of things at the plant, very much on top, already confident with success. Already the top-echelon men at the factory were replacing his city friends in his dinner-table monologues and, so far as she could tell, in his affections. He had found a good barber, a satisfactory place to lunch and a quiet bar for a five o'clock drink. At home he was happy and undemanding, asking only that she appreciate him. True, Sunday was coming up and he would probably start fumbling at her before she got the dinner dishes stacked, but she could stand it.

She shut her eyes and leaned her head back against the slippery upholstery, thinking about a slender sad-faced girl with fair hair and a light way of walking.

I'll find her, she thought, smiling a little, and next time I'll be myself. I'll find some way to let her know.

4 SHE LAY AWAKE FOR A LONG TIME AFTER BILL rolled over to his own side of the bed, turned his face to the wall and began to snore. The male smell was on her, the events of the last half hour were clear in her mind, yet it all

seemed unreal, like something seen in the movies. She thought, I really am a whore. And she didn't care.

At last she got up, too restless to lie still anymore and afraid that her turning would wake Bill. She showered, put on her old terry robe, and went downstairs, feeling her way along stair railings and groping for doorknobs in the still-unfamiliar house. Under the bright overhead light of the kitchen she made coffee and sat writing shopping lists while it perked. Things she needed for the house: a sofa, rugs, curtains, a telephone stand. Things she needed for herself: a light jacket, gloves, shampoo. In the morning she would read it all over and decide how much of it made sense; she always felt wide-awake and alert at this hour, but in the light of day her ideas sometimes looked quite different.

She knew, in the back of her mind, why she was doing all this. With a handful of lists she had a valid reason for going downtown in the morning, and while she was there she would visit the bookstore. That was what she had been waiting for all through Friday night, Saturday and Sunday—might as well admit it. She set down her empty cup and looked blindly out of the window.

She was setting out to look for a girl she had seen only once, a girl who had no reason to be interested in her; who might even, if they met again, actively dislike her. No reason she shouldn't.

She put all the lists in her purse and picked her way back to bed. The radium dial of her clock said one twenty. She lay thinking about Erika's greenish-gray eyes. Did they slant a little or didn't they? Something gave her a slightly exotic look, piquant with that fair hair. She fell asleep trying to make up her mind.

Bill looked a little guilty at breakfast and a little resentful too, like a man who has been accused of something he didn't do but would have liked to. He said, "It's going to be a hot day," and she said, scorning the weather, "I'm going downtown to look at some furniture. All right?"

"Better fix yourself some breakfast then."

"I'm not hungry."

"You don't need to diet. You women are all crazy when it comes to weight."

"That's right."

He looked at her, unsatisfied but finding nothing to argue with.

She put on an old cotton skirt, plain shirt and loafers, office clothes left over from the days when she was Bake's girl—not to be confused with Mrs. William Ollenfield. Pushing the hangers along her closet bar and looking with distaste at her wardrobe, she wondered what had ever possessed her to buy so many clothes she didn't like. Mrs. William Ollenfield seemed to be the sort of woman who goes shopping in a hat and gloves, who wears little printed silks and puts scatter pins on the lapel of a suit. Sooner or later, she would want and get a fur coat. Frances faced herself in the long mirror.

She was no longer certain who she was or what she might hope to become, but she certainly didn't intend to spend the rest of her life pretending to be Mrs. William Ollenfield, that smug little housewife. She didn't even like the way the woman did her hair. She ran a wet comb through the lacquered curls, smacked down the resulting fuzz with a brush dipped in Bill's hair stuff, and caught the subdued ends in a barrette. The plain styling brought out the oval shape of her face and the winged eyebrows, her only beauty. (Not quite the only one, Bake had argued, touching her lightly to remind her.) Now she was beginning to look like herself again.

She ran downstairs, relishing the freedom of bare legs and old shapeless loafers.

It was one of those lazy summer days that seem endless, with sunlight clear and golden over the world and great patches of shade under arching branches. Grass and trees still wore the bright green of early summer. People moved along with open, friendly faces, looking washed and ironed. She climbed aboard a fat yellow bus and handed the driver a dollar, not wanting to admit that she didn't know what the fare was. He gave back eighty-five cents.

She saw now that at some point during the weekend she had

ceased to take for granted the continued backing of the Ollen-field income. She felt free and self-reliant. She wasn't sure why, but no doubt she would find out in time.

In front of the bookstore, however, she lost her courage. She stood looking into the display window, which was just as it had been on Friday except for a small ivory Madonna where her wooden cat had been. As long as she didn't go in, anything was possible. But if she went in and Vince wasn't there, or if he was cool to her or refused to tell her about Erika—well, she reminded herself, I won't be any worse off than I was this time last week. Back where I started from.

But she knew she would have lost something important. A hope so new and fragile she dared not examine it.

She turned the knob and went in.

The fair girl was sitting on a folding chair at the back of the room, writing on a clipboard. She looked up as Frances came in, heralded by the little silvery bell. Several expressions crossed her face—recognition, surprise, terror. She stood up, holding the clipboard stiffly at her side. "Vince. Customer."

A voice from somewhere in the back. "Don't forget what I said."

"Vince says that I owe you an apology. I'm sorry I was rude."

"But you weren't rude. You were terribly polite."

"That's what Vince said. There is a rude kind of politeness."

"I know, you use it on people you don't like. But there's no reason you should like me," Frances admitted. "You don't even know me. I have no business going around asking strangers out for drinks—"

"I keep telling her," Vince said, coming in elegantly from a back room, dirty hands held out in front of him, "you either like people or you don't, and why wait for a formal introduction? Personally," he said airily, "I always know the first time I meet somebody, and I hardly ever change my mind. I must say this is an improvement over that terrible dress you had on the other time, though."

Frances was too embarrassed to answer. Vince came to a graceful stop between her and Erika. "It's my day for apologies

24

too," he said nicely. "I didn't get your name and address when you were here, or ask you what kind of books you were interested in. You left your packages, too."

"Frances Ollenfield."

"This is Erika Frohmann. Now you've been introduced. You can be rude to each other if you want to."

He retreated into the back again. There was the sound of running water. Erika Frohmann seemed to be gathering up her courage. "I'm not very good at meeting people," she said, looking not at Frances but at the floor. "And you reminded me of someone too. Not a parent."

"I look like a million other people."

Vince emerged again, drying his hands on a small grimy towel. "Don't be modest, my dear. You have a lovely profile— now you've done away with those dreadful, horrible curls. If I didn't give my customers a little shove they might never get acquainted. They're such a small group I feel they ought to know one another."

Frances said, "I like small groups." Take off your mask, let me see if you know. They wouldn't, of course. Even if they wondered, caution was an hourly habit. She asked, hot faced, "Is it all right if I look at the books?"

"Sure, go ahead. You can wash your hands when you get through."

Erika Frohmann said defensively, "Paper gets so dirty." She sat down again, but tentatively, propping her clipboard against the edge of a counter and plainly trying to think of something to write. Her apology made and accepted, if only tacitly, the conversation was apparently over as far as she was concerned.

Frances walked slowly to the shelves, conscious of the silent figure behind her. But the fascination of print took over. Bake had long ago introduced her to secondhand bookstores on Clark Street and Dearborn, a wonderful clutter of junk and treasure, with the three-for-a-dollar bins just outside their doors and tables of old tattered paperbacks just inside. She was still unable to pass a secondhand bookstore.

This place was small, but there was enough to keep her here

all day. She walked slowly, picking up volumes as she went along, now and then putting one back, scrupulously, where it had been in the first place.

Here were the Ann Bannon books side-by-side with Jeanette Foster's *Sex Variant Women in Literature*, *North Beach Girl*, and *Take Me Home* next to the Covici-Friede edition of *The Well of Loneliness*, dated 1928. Here, huddled together as though for warmth in an unfriendly world, were Gore Vidal and a tall thin volume of Baudelaire, translated by someone she had never heard of. Here were books in the field, for people with a special interest, a special orientation.

Her voice came out shrill with self-consciousness. "Are these for sale?"

Vince came to see what she was talking about. "That depends. Why do you want them?"

Now. Tell him. But she could only say, "I've read most of them, but there are some I don't know."

He looked at her. The right answer evidently showed on her face; he nodded. "I'll ask Erika. A lot of them belong to her. She may want them back."

Erika stood up, soundless in flat canvas shoes. He said, indicating Frances with his thumb, "Can she have your books?"

"What for?"

"I thought you wanted to get rid of them. That was the general idea of bringing them here, wasn't it?"

"But not to just anybody."

Frances waited. The books are here to be sold, she thought, this is a bookstore. Why are they on display if they're not for sale? But she said nothing. Something more was involved—this was a matter with deep emotional implications, and anything she said was likely to be wrong. It was the boy, Vince, who said with an impatient edge to his voice, "You can have them back if you've changed your mind. Go on, take them home with you."

Erika's face was hard and cold. She looked at Frances. "Let her take them if she wants. But not for money."

"Look, we went through this with the insurance money."

"It's the same thing."

Vince said to Frances, "It's not just curiosity, is it? You won't pass them around for your friends to laugh at?"

Frances said steadily, daring everything now, "If I had any friends here, they'd be interested for different reasons."

Vince smiled. "Okay, they're yours. No charge. Get them out of Erika's way. She likes to come here and brood."

Erika put the clipboard down on the counter, carefully, as though it might shatter. She walked soundlessly out of the store. The chimes over the door jingled. A streak of sunlight flashed across the floor and was gone.

Vince took the half dozen assorted books Frances was holding, since she seemed unable to put them down. "Don't look that way. I wasn't trying to hurt your feelings."

"It's her feelings."

"Her best friend was killed. I told you." The graceful shrug was as much a part of him as his clear brown eyes. "Girls are so sentimental. You have to go on living, and sooner or later you find someone else. It's a little soon for her, that's all."

Frances said in a whisper, "I like her."

"Sure. She's had a bad time. She's an Austrian, she was in a concentration camp when she was eleven, twelve years old, I don't know exactly. Her whole family was murdered. I think it took all the courage she had to really love anyone—I think Kate was the only person she ever gave a damn about. If Kate had lived they would have stayed together forever like an old married couple. She's a monogamous type," Vince said, apparently not considering monogamy much of a virtue.

Frances opened one of the paperbacks to hide her confusion. The name, Kate Wood, was written strongly across the top of the title page in black ink. She said, "Some people would have kept these, and grieved over them."

"Erika's very strong. It would be better if she yelled and fainted," Vince said sadly. "I love her. Not in an erotic way, of course."

Frances said, "I think I could love her, period."

"You're gay."

"Yes."

27

"Doing anything about it?"

"Not right now."

"You should never admit you're gay," Vince said quietly, "people have such fantastic ideas. You have to wear a disguise most of the time—if somebody finds out!" He drew a finger across his throat. "It's worse for us, though."

"I believe you."

He lifted graceful shoulders. "So keep the books. Erika won't take money for them. It's a superstition, like the women who won't cash their children's insurance policies. We went through that, too. Kate had a group policy where she worked, made out to Erika as the beneficiary. Erika paid the funeral expenses out of it and gave the rest away. She's terribly hard up, she never has any money, but that's what she wanted to do."

"I can see how she felt."

"Yeah, but couldn't she see that Kate wanted to leave her provided for? She hasn't got a nickel saved. What happens if she gets sick and can't work?"

I'd take care of her, Frances thought, warming. I'd work my hands off to take care of her.

"She gave away all Kate's clothes and all the furniture and stuff they had and moved into a furnished room. I don't know what it's like, I've never been there. As far as I know nobody has. I've got a key, she gave it to me when she got out of the hospital—she was afraid of dying in her sleep," Vince said matter-of-factly. "She was supposed to call me up every day, and if she missed a day I was supposed to check. But she never missed. You don't just walk in on Erika."

Frances wondered if it were a warning. She said, "I'll take care of the books. Maybe she'll want them back some time."

"I don't know why she didn't keep them."

Frances knew. Books have a life of their own. She felt warm and tender, as though she were melting with compassion. She said with some difficulty, "Tell her I took them, will you? And tell her—"

"With some things, you have to do your own telling."

"Yes. Of course. Can I take some of these now and come back for the rest?"

"Any time, sure. Wash your hands before you go."

Out in the street, she looked around with some surprise. For a while she had forgotten where she was—and who she was supposed to be. Maybe, she thought, I can start being myself again. She stood uncertainly in the middle of the sidewalk, holding the heavy package Vince had tied for her: ten, and she could pick up the rest a few at a time. She had a good reason to go back.

Furniture, she thought dimly, finding her crumpled lists as she hunted for tissues in her handbag. She didn't want to shop. She wanted to go somewhere and think about Erika Frohmann. She wanted to talk to Kay, who was in Iran by this time and out of her reach since there are some things you can't say in letters.

Vaguely, with nothing better to do, she made her way to Shapiro's and roamed through the furniture department on the top floor, looking at things without seeing them, until her package became too heavy.

What difference did it make how she furnished the house? It wasn't her house, never would be. She wasn't going to stay in it. But she realized that she would have to account for the day to Bill.

She had forgotten Bill, too. For a couple of hours he had stopped existing.

She stood in front of a French Provincial chest, looking beyond it, holding her packet of books as though it were a child.

5 IN THE DAYS WHERE FRANCES WAS STILL FRANKIE Kirby, the pindling half-fed child of a soft-coal miner, the district was the heart of her small world, not the company house where her ailing mother dragged from washtub to dishpan to cookstove, or the mine where her father disappeared every morning, to emerge grimed and sullen at night. For Frances Ollenfield, married to a young man more and more absorbed in business, it lay inside the covers of books—a vicar-

ious life that ranged from Jane Austen to Kerouac. And later, everything important was concentrated in the apartment where she and Bake had so much happiness—and then, at the end, so much bitterness.

Now she had no center, and she was incomplete and fragmented. More and more, as the days passed, she found herself thinking about Erika Frohmann. The girl was becoming an obsession, the focal point in a life that had grown increasingly meaningless. She longed to take Erika in her arms and comfort her for all the evil which life had brought her. Her arms ached, her breasts ached for the pressure of Erika's body.

To a bystander, the life of Mrs. William Ollenfield at this time was centered in the big square layer-cake house on Regent Street. She threw herself into the furnishing and decorating of the rooms, drowning her needs in work. She bought a table and sofa, three chairs, rugs and curtains and numerous small things for the living room, ending with something that looked like an illustration from *Home Beautiful*. It wasn't a décor that encouraged blue jeans and bare feet—but of course Mrs. William Ollenfield wore shoes even when she was alone in the house.

She even talked to Bill about fixing up the basement for parties, a step that seemed to have special meaning for him—a status symbol, she thought scornfully, like the backyard barbeque and the car with tail fins. A place to give parties. That she disliked parties didn't make any difference, people gave them anyway, and the other guests probably disliked them too. But one had to go.

She fitted up one of the bedrooms as a guest room, with light, functional furniture and flowered curtains; the effect pleased her. It occurred to her that she would like to move into it herself, away from Bill's nightly tossings and his twice-a-week fumbling and the male smell of him. It would be a place where she could sleep deeply, not intruded upon, not violated. But if she left Bill's bed she would have to leave his house as well, and she wasn't ready for that decisive step. Not just yet.

She didn't know where the idea of leaving had come from. It seemed to spring up in her mind from some long-dormant root, putting out leaves and blossoms at an astonishing rate. She waited to see what that fruit might be.

In the meanwhile, to pass the time and keep herself from becoming tense with wondering, she went on buying things and putting them in place, creating an effect of comfort not like a housewife building her own nest, but like the manager of a hotel, paid to do what she did. She felt no involvement. She would never live here, or not long enough to make any difference. It was no home of hers.

She thought about it, soaking in the bathtub an hour before the Wives were due for cards and coffee. It was the feeling that goes with working out two weeks' notice on a job, already emotionally separated and impatient to leave. Between two worlds and accountable to neither. In this frame of mind she had called up the Wives, putting an end to Bill's nagging; she faced their arrival calmly because they were not and never would be a part of her life. It cost nothing to be polite to them.

She dressed for the Wives with great care, put on a dress with flowers on it, did her hair the way Bill liked it. Going downstairs, she felt a flash of proud pleasure. The house was spotless. She had made a date torte, more impressive than a layer cake and really no more difficult. She was safe.

The night before she had lain awake sick to her stomach with fright, hoping she might be coming down with something spotty and contagious so she could call off the party. But when the doorbell rang, she went calmly to let the first two in, the freckled redhead and a small blonde who kept throwing bits of baby talk French into the conversation. They were laughing, but in a nice way, a social way. The redhead said, "I adore the way you've fixed this place up. I want to do my living room over but Joe keeps saying not this year—"

It was easy. She was one of them, for the time being. If you were married to an executive and had your hair done professionally and never, never said anything you really thought, you were in. For what it was worth. I can be charming as all hell when I want to, she thought, hiding a giggle.

Four hours later, standing at the front door to let them out, she wondered why she had worried. It had been easy—knowing that it wasn't going to last, it had even been fun. Things are only difficult when you care, she thought, pleased. She could play it cool with these pleasant women because she wasn't going to be doing it forever. She was going to get out.

The conviction lingered in the days that followed, even though events seemed to stand still. July deepened into hotter sunshine and richer growth, the grass in the backyard darkened and thickened, the humming of insects filled the late afternoons. Frances discovered a simple pleasure she had forgotten since the first years of her marriage: sitting outdoors alone after nightfall, breathing the cool grassy fragrance that follows a hot, humid day. Bill was often out, as he had been on the other job; his busyness gave her a chance to breathe. She took an old leather cushion out on the grass and sat relaxed, idle yet aware, breathing in the summer nights.

The old couple next door sat on their front porch, in a plastic glider with creaking joints. When they went in she usually sat for a while relishing her aloneness, looking at the moon and the little drifting clouds and listening to the tree branches making the same gentle sighing they had made in Shakespeare's England. "On such a night as this," she thought, standing up, cushion in hand, as the next-door television came to life. No soft summer evening would keep the old people from going in to listen to Floyd Dalber's newscast on channel five, after which they would go placidly to bed.

It didn't seem to her that the news could be regarded as soporific, but at least it made a break in the day. She usually drank a last cup of coffee and went to bed around half past ten because there was nothing else to do.

Going to bed didn't necessarily mean going to sleep, however. Bill had installed a window air-conditioner in the bedroom; next year, if he took over the house, he would have the whole place air-conditioned, sealed away from the living, breathing outdoors. The unit made a hypnotic whirring whisper that sent her into a half-drowse for an hour or so. Then she was awake, sweating with tension in the artificial coolness, and lonely to desolation.

Bake, she thought, turning and moving on the bed as though her hungry body might touch another in its need. But Bake was part of a past that was irretrievably gone. She didn't want to think about Bake in terms of the present, driving swiftly with Jane beside her in the car, waking on Sunday mornings to hear Jane moving around quietly in the kitchen, or—Frances drew a sharp breath—peeling off her shirt and slacks in the white moonlight that flowed through the bedroom window, while Jane lay in bed watching her with wide eyes and a waiting smile. That hurt.

It was better to think about the future. At least, it would have been better if she could have foreseen any future. There was no predictable end to the hunger for love that tore her in pieces, these hot summer nights.

In the daytime she was hungry for two things: something to do that had meaning, someone who offered companionship. At night she was kept awake by a craving that only one thing would satisfy. There were things she could do for herself, but which filled no real need, which only eased the physical tensions for a while. She scorned them as childish. I need someone to love, she thought in misery.

It was worse when Bill felt amorous. After he fell asleep she got up and bathed, brushed her teeth and shampooed her hair as though hot water could dissolve his touch. She didn't hate him; sitting on the edge of the tub, rubbing her head with a thick towel, she wondered why that realization made her feel worse instead of better. Hell, I don't even dislike him. He's a nice guy. I wouldn't mind being his secretary; he'd be a nice boss, kind about days off and small raises. I just don't want him to touch me. I don't want any man to touch me.

That's what marriage is, though. It makes an obligation out of a free gift. I want—

I want a lot of things, she concluded, pulling a fresh nightgown over her head. (Bill liked her in nightgowns, preferably sheer nylon ones with lace. Left to herself she slept in cotton pajamas. Bake had wanted her naked.) A lot of things I'm not going to get in a hurry.

She smoothed the sheets and got decorously back into bed, lying well away from Bill and pulling her gown down as far as she could. Bill was sleeping out loud, his mouth open a little. The top sheet was pushed down around his legs, and the chest and groin hairs were beaded with sweat. She felt repulsed and pitying at the same time. A nice guy, as far as he knew how to be. He had taken her back and been kind to her—as far as he knew how to be. He even wanted to buy her a fur coat, she reminded herself, closing her eyes and composing her face for sleep, although she knew she wasn't going to get any sleep for the next few hours.

The problem was that she didn't want a fur coat, or a new sofa and wall-to-wall broadloom, or even (smothering a nervous snicker), the pure love of a good man. No, nor fifteen minutes of his valuable attention twice a week. She wanted someone to love. It wouldn't be a man, no matter how kind and generous he was. To make love with a man seemed to her a kind of perversion.

Bill stirred in his sleep. She lay still on the front edge of the bed, watching the shadows move along the wall as late cars rolled down the street.

It was almost morning when she fell into an uneasy half-sleep broken by street sounds and the heat of Bill's body so close to hers. She dreamed of Erika.

The alarm clock woke her, not tired now but strangely rested and clear in her mind. It was a fine, hot, sunny day. She got up and stood looking out of the bedroom window, hearing Bill thumping around in the bathroom; he was the kind of man who jumps out of bed at the first buzz and goes into high gear immediately. The old man next door was already out, placing the sprinkler so his flowers would get the good of the water before the sun was high. He looked busy and contented. She beamed at him from behind her curtain.

She was going to find Erika Frohmann.

She didn't know what would happen after that, but anything would be better than these long nights full of needing.

6

IT WAS LIKE THE FIRST DAY AT COUNTY HIGH, standing in front of the big brick building in her stiff homemade gingham, watching the town girls go up the sidewalk in giggling groups as though they owned the place. It was like waiting for polio shots with nobody to tell her, as she used to tell Bob, that it would be over in just a minute. It was like getting ready to have her first baby, with an aching back and nausea and deepening panic. She was scared.

It was like standing just outside the doors of youth, watching them swing shut against her. She had felt this unreasoning panic once before, on her thirtieth birthday.

She gathered up all her courage, opened the door of the bookstore and went in, not hearing the silver tinkle of the bells because her ears were thick with terror.

Erika Frohmann was standing beside the cash register, her elbows propped on the wooden counter, her blonde head bent over a magazine. She looked up. The polite inquiry on her face gave way to recognition. She said, "Hi. Vince has expected you."

"Oh—the rest of the books."

"Also he likes you."

From which she knew that Vince had told Erika the one thing she had to know. She said, keeping her voice even, "I like him too. Do you work here?"

"Not really. I'm only watching the store while he goes out. I have nothing to do in the summer, you see."

"Would you like to go out for breakfast, or something, when he gets back?"

Erika said, "I'd like coffee. Thank you very much."

They looked at each other. Before Frances could think of anything else to say—she who had been so glib with the Wives only yesterday—Vince came in, walking light and catlike in Moroccan slippers turned up at the toes. Erika slipped out from behind the counter. "We're going for coffee," she said, and Vince grinned, pleased. "All right, I'll see both of you later."

So they were walking down the hot street side-by-side, their steps nicely matched. Frances felt lightheaded with pleasure.

Erika's face looked less boyish in the sunshine; she had the shadowed eyes and hollow cheeks of one who lies awake night after night, remembering. She said, smiling a little, "Vince is very nice. Some people might not like him because—you know, he has his own problems."

"Because he's gay," Frances said hopefully. The word was so out of keeping with Erika's rather melancholy expression that she couldn't help smiling. "It's a silly word."

"It is. I can't think of anything less gay than being gay." She gave Frances a small inquiring look from under cautious half-closed eyelids. Frances nodded.

"Vince said so. I thought—"

"He asked me."

"The other words are worse, anyway."

"You can't always tell about people, the way they dress and everything. It's embarrassing to make a mistake."

"Especially if you start late. Then, too, this is a foreign country for me even now. The customs are different."

"Did you start late?" She was sorry she had asked; Erika's face set in a pattern of stern sorrow. Too late Frances remembered what Vince had told her about this girl's past.

"Only three, in all my life. And the first two were not so important. I can't go in bars like a man looking for a whore," Erika said proudly. "It has to be everything—or not at all. The mind and the inside thoughts, doesn't that belong with love too?"

"The same with me. Maybe only one matters. Maybe it's never the same with anyone else."

Erika said abruptly, "Here is a good place for coffee. I found it a few weeks ago."

It was a small cheap-looking restaurant, brightly lighted and rather noisy. "No air-conditioning and no Muzak. Do you mind?"

"I hate air-conditioning and Muzak."

"So do I. Also things made of plastic. And commercials on television."

"And the poetry in newspapers, like prose only with dots to show where the lines are."

"You hate the right things," Erika said, smiling. She settled back in the booth and stretched a little, as though she were tired. Her face looked drawn in the light, the skin too tight over the cheekbones. Frances said, "Don't talk if you don't want to. It's so hot."

Erika said simply, "I don't sleep."

"Neither do I."

"Nobody sleeps any more. It's out of style. People take pills to put themselves to sleep, and different pills to wake themselves up."

The waitress said, smiling, "Hello, Miss Frohmann. Coffee? A sweet roll or something?"

"Only coffee, please."

They were silent as they waited. It wasn't like being with Bake, who always had a dozen things to share and who talked well. But it was pleasant. Time to stop thinking about Bake, that was over. She looked at Erika. Erika's eyes were a light gray-green, flecked like agate. Her eyelashes curled like a baby's. She wore no makeup at all, and a few freckles spattered her nose and cheeks. She sighed, pushing her hair back from a forehead that was beginning to show faint lines.

"Vince wants me to ask you to a meeting. Only if you want to, you don't have to come," Erika said when their coffee was before them in thick green-banded cups. She looked at the steam rising in delicate spirals. "You take it black? So do I."

"What kind of a meeting?"

"A group for people like us. We have speakers and book reviews—like what are our legal rights, and how can we get better jobs? You don't need to be afraid, it has nothing to do with the communists," she added with a little smile. "Everyone in this country is afraid of communists. I don't know why, there can't be so many—I don't know a single one."

"Neither do I."

"This is a good way to meet people," Erika said, as though Frances hadn't fretted through weeks of hot summer nights over just that. "You may have seen the magazine. It's called *Others*."

"Oh." She had heard about this organization, at Bake's place and over the beer at Karla's. Kay approved. Bake was scornful of it. "A lot of butches and bitches. God knows what they find to talk about. It's the American mania for joining things, that's all. Besides, who wants to get on a mailing list?"

"The last young man Vince asked was so disappointed. He expected orgies. We're very serious."

Frances said weakly, "It sounds interesting." It didn't—and how would she account for her evening to Bill?

Erika's laugh was unexpectedly deep. "Passing resolutions and answering letters? Someone has to do it. It is nice to sit and drink coffee with people who know what you are, that's all."

"I think I'd like to." Because how else was she to see Erika again? That was all that mattered at this point.

"Good. There is a meeting at Vince's apartment on Friday night. Next Friday, eight o'clock. I'll write the number for you."

"Could I pick you up?"

"No, I'll go early." She found a pencil in her pocket, started to tear a margin off the magazine she had put down, then changed her mind and handed Frances the whole thing, with the address written in a small foreign-looking script along the top. "This is the national magazine. Take it if you want to."

It was a small publication, sixteen pages, about six-by-eight inches, neatly printed and decorated with pen and ink sketches. Frances hadn't known that such a thing existed. She said, "Thanks, I'll bring it back when I'm done with it."

Frances had known about the bars, yes; from her reading she knew that Karla's and the Gay Eighties had their counterparts everywhere. New York was famous for them, the west coast was supposed to be a paradise for pickups (at least, between spasmodic raids when the police exchequer was low or public feeling ran high); Paris, Vienna, Madrid, everywhere you went, said the travelers, you found the "different" ones, ready to recognize and welcome their own. They ranged from park and washroom pickups to the sober hard-working couples pledged to monogamy and permanence. It was a world within a world, of whose very existence most people were unaware. To Frances it was a comforting thought.

She had never enjoyed barhopping. She remembered the evenings she had spent sitting bored and tired, drinking too much, waiting for Bake to be ready to go home. But where else can you meet people? She thought of all the women going home to furnished rooms after their day's work, wishing they had someone to love but forever outside the world of man-woman loving (as though that were not capable of infinite variations), lonely and hungry and not knowing how to look for companionship. And then there were the lucky ones who stumbled upon fulfillment, as she had done with Bake, and sometimes went on for years, warmed by a lasting love. Not many, but a few.

This might be one way to an answer—an organization, a magazine. For lonely girls in small towns, in colleges, in impersonal cities, at least the reassurance that there were others. She said abruptly, "While you're talking about hating the right things—I hate that word. Homosexual. It sounds like a disease."

"Some people think it is," Erika said sadly. "The psychologists have one, homophile. Like something that could put you in a violent ward. Or in jail."

"It's been known to happen."

"Lesbian isn't so bad."

"Bad enough. What do you say?"

Erika smiled. "I say so-and-so, whatever the person's name is. I prefer to think about people. You like string beans, I like spinach, does this keep people from being people?"

"That's good if you can do it. Like not thinking some things are masculine and others feminine, as if anybody were entirely one or the other. Why do people make an issue of it?"

"What other people do doesn't matter."

The cups were empty. They sat looking at each other. Everybody always talks about the subject, Frances thought, let two gay kids get together and they start reviewing the whole history of homosexuality. Like the jokes about the Polish question. Of course it's a social issue, kind of. But right now—

Right now she wanted Erika.

Erika stood up, composed and neat. There was nothing to do but follow her out, stopping at the cashier's desk to pay the check.

Nobody could ever own this one, she thought, standing beside Erika in the doorway. But she could give a lot if she really cared. She hasn't cared for many people. And she's been terribly hurt.

"Are you coming back to Vince's?" she asked.

"Not today."

"I'd like to see you again."

"Of course. Friday at eight."

But that wasn't what she meant.

She stood alone on the sidewalk, watching Erika walk down the street. We could be friends, she told herself, cheered by the rapport that had already developed between them. But friendship was only part of what she wanted.

She knew she couldn't rush things with this girl. She wasn't like Bake, definite, aggressive, ready to come into your arms in a burst of feeling. This one had been hurt. She kept herself locked away. It would be necessary to go slowly.

She walked back to the bookstore, feeling that Vince, at least, would listen with sympathy. But he had a paying customer who seemed in no hurry to leave. She picked up another armful of books and left, feeling frustrated.

She didn't think she was hard hearted. She had felt sorry for a lot of people. Bob, when he lay spotted and feverish with measles or chicken pox. Lissa, whose heart broke every time she ended an affair—and was healed with a smile. Kay, in the quiet grief of her love's ending—frightened and heartsick as she herself had been when Bake and Jane began their slow inevitable drift together. She and Kay had shared their renunciation.

But she had never felt about anyone as she did about Erika Frohmann; and that, she knew, was because her compassion was mixed with desire. The silent dignity of Erika's loneliness, as though she had endured it silently for a long time, filled her with a physical hurt. The palms of her hands ached, her throat tightened. For the first time she wanted to take someone in her arms and give all she had, with no thought of her own fulfillment.

She told herself she was being romantic and silly. She went back to the house on Regent Street, and the door opened to let her in. The rooms were cool and spacious—and empty. She had no place there.

She cooked the evening meal and sat across the table from Bill, eating without knowing what was on her plate, saying yes and no to Bill's latest installment of what they were doing at the plant. In her mind was a picture of a girl with gray-green eyes and freckled cheeks. It was a kind of love she had never felt before, but she had no doubt that it was love.

7 BILL SAID, "WE OUGHT TO HAVE A PARTY."

Frances's book slithered off her lap. She picked it up, spreading her fingers protectively over the title.

"The Wives were just here for lunch and cards."

"I mean a real party. Some of the people I've been meeting on my job. It's time we started following up some of these contacts."

She knew what he had in mind, the old status climb, but she was damned if she was going to say it for him. She sat waiting, with her book open on her lap.

"Everybody's been pretty nice to us. It might be fun to have some people in."

Can this marriage last? Read the *Ladies Companion* and find out how this little woman kept her husband's love by becoming a gracious hostess. Husbands, let your wives know you appreciate their bird-brained achievements. They sit around the house all day while you work your fingers to the bone, dictating letters and drinking martinis on the expense account.

But she felt an unwilling pride. After all, the house did look good, and she had the blisters to prove it. She said, "All right, if you want to. I just thought—you're often out in the evening."

"For Christ sake, I can take a night off, can't I?"

It didn't matter. Except that every nice thing she did now was going to make it worse for him when she left at last.

"I suppose you think I never think about anything but business," Bill said defensively. "What's wrong with that? The fellows at the office are all right. And you get along with the girls, don't you?"

That was the truth, Frances realized miserably. They were good people, even kind people—as long as they figured you for their kind. Admit that you're a little different and you'll be crucified. Why couldn't he understand that she would never belong?

It was no use. Her year of hard work, following their reconciliation, had succeeded in one way: Bill now thought of her affair with Bake as an aberration, an unpleasant but temporary interruption to a happy, normal marriage. She had played Mrs. Ollenfield so skillfully that she had Mr. Ollenfield completely fooled. He knew, manwise, that women do wacky things. Other men's wives carried on with men or drank too much or had to be hospitalized with nervous breakdowns. She had wronged him, too, but with great nobility he had forgiven (but not forgotten) and taken her back into his bed. As far as he was concerned the incident was closed.

He was going to be so surprised when he found out.

As far as she was concerned, it wasn't the three years with Bake that were evil, but the return to unlove. To accept forgiveness for an episode she didn't think was wrong—that was really immoral. She was twice as guilty as he thought, but not for the reason he had in mind.

Bill turned back to his figuring. She closed the book and sat with her eyes half shut, trying to come to some meaningful conclusion and failing, as usual. Thoughts of Bake obsessed her lately. Not the Bake of their last unhappy days together, drunk and antagonistic, but the girl who had first taught her the ways of love.

They had come in tired and dirty from a heavenly day in the autumn woods, and Bake had built a blaze in the fireplace. Sitting side-by-side on the wide couch with the hand-loomed Indian spread, they drifted into talk. Until, at last, Bake had the courage to mention what was in both their minds. Frances could guess now what that initial approach had cost Bake, in her proud determination never to bring a straight girl out; least of all a woman with a husband and half-grown son. Bake had weighed the chance of failure and her own belief that she was doing wrong. But at the time she hadn't known that.

She could feel again, thrilling all through her body, the fright and compulsive longing that struggled in her as Bake undressed her and lay down beside her. The panic that swept over her at the first touch of Bake's hands on her naked body, a woman's hands for the first time rousing her to desire. And, too, a new pride because Bake found her attractive. Bake's hands and lips, and the gradual rise to a crest of feeling that was mixed with fear before she finally let go and the wild explosion swept her into a different world.

This is it, she thought just before the tide swept her away. This is what I always wanted and never knew. She heard herself making low moaning sounds like an animal in distress, heard the soft scream rise in her throat as the fulfillment became more than she could bear.

And, oh God, the joy of waking in the early morning with Bake's body lying warm and solid against her, knowing that this marvelous person loved her and was pleased to make her happy. At that moment, growing out of her new-found peace and joy like a flower unfolding, had come the thought: I can learn to do all this for her, I can give her pleasure back again. It filled her with a new confidence.

Frances moved uneasily, slanting a look at Bill who sat jotting down columns of figures. It had been so long. She had tried to forget. And now things she thought she had forgotten kept crowding into her memory—the memory that lives in muscles and nerve endings. Desire rose in her like a fountain.

Her love for Bake was the only completely good thing she'd

ever had. And this man sitting at his desk, looking things up in *Dun and Bradstreet*, saw it as something abnormal and evil. I can never tell him, she thought. He'll never understand. And he has had such a wonderful time forgiving me and taking me back. She looked at him coldly, seeing him as a stranger.

Because of course Kay was right. There was no doubt in her mind, after a year of "happy normal marriage." She was a lesbian. (Names again.) The three years with Bake hadn't been an experiment, but a revelation of the truth about herself. She had denied it. She had tried to change—but does anyone ever change? Isn't your true basic self alive as long as you live, hidden away, beaten down, but always ready to come alive at a word or scent or a remembered bit of music?

It was the reunion with Bill that had been an experiment—and it was a failure. For a year she'd done everything he wanted her to do, tried to be everything he asked her to be, restricted her life to the four walls of his house and her behavior to the decidedly stuffy ideas with which he had grown up. She had even tried to be grateful to him. A pushover for a little kindness, she thought in scorn of her softness. She couldn't go on this way.

Bill looked up. "How about it, Fran? It wouldn't be so much work. You could have a woman in to help. You could have somebody all the time if you felt like it, I'm making enough. That's why I work so hard, so you can have things and Bob can finish his degree work."

"Sure. We can have a party. If you want one so badly."

"What's the matter, don't you want to?"

She tried to smile. "You know I'm never at my best in a crowd."

"It wouldn't have to be more than four or five couples."

Oh, the animals came in two by two. A man for me and a girl for you. Suppose she said, "All right, can I invite my girl?"

But of course she didn't have a girl. Yet. She was building all her plans on the weakest of foundations.

"We could have a catered affair. You wouldn't even have to step into the kitchen. Most of these people are poker players, no job to entertain them. I could pick up a couple party records—no rough stuff, just an icebreaker. We'll have fun, Fran."

She stood up, a finger between the pages of her book. "All right. I'm going to bed, if you don't mind. I'm tired."

"It's all right about the party, isn't it? I don't want to push you into anything you don't want to do."

Damn him. Now she couldn't even feel like a martyr. She said slowly, "Sure, you ought to entertain the people who've been nice to you, that's a good idea. I'll think of a good menu."

"I'm not doing it just for myself."

Same old record, same old groove, same old dull needle. She waited. He said politely, "What are you reading?"

"Paperback I picked up. It doesn't amount to much."

He swiveled back to his work. She climbed the stairs slowly, holding the book against the folds of her skirt.

The book was one of those she had kept hidden in the attic, the boxful she hadn't been able to throw away even at the hour of her greatest determination to conform. She had put them away, promising herself that some day, when she was brave enough, she would take that box out and burn it. Now the contents seemed like a promise of better times to come. All those books "in the field"—Bannon, Cory, Aldrich, Hall, Taylor, Wilhelm, Foster, as well as the classics—said to her, "You are not alone." From time to time, when she was safely alone in the house, she chose a title and plunged into the life she thought she had left behind forever.

The book she held now was one of Erika's. Reading it made Frances feel closer to her. At least, she thought, Erika had been spared the disillusionment that comes when love ends, both parties trying to save a feeling that no longer has meaning.

Upstairs, she undressed quickly in the master bedroom, now so interior decorated that it had no character at all unless she left things lying around. She threw her bra and lacy half-slip over the back of a chair and, turning on the overhead light, looked critically at herself in the mirror. She had always felt she was too thin. Now, with middle age approaching and many of her acquaintances crammed into tight girdles, she was glad. I may not be bosomy enough to suit Bill, she thought—he liked the Playboy type—but she wasn't unhappy about that. She put her hands under her breasts and was pleased at their firmness and instant response to her touch.

She got into bed and opened her book. A soft peach light glowed through the shade of the reading lamp on the night table. When she got drowsy she could drop the book down behind the bed, to keep it out of Bill's sight.

She was used to being alone. Over the last few years, Bill's evening routine had settled into a pattern on the few evenings he spent at home: he would work until midnight or later, making out reports and reading other reports, correlating sales figures, typing things on his little German portable with the nervous chattering keys that kept her awake. Around eleven the sound of typing would stop while he made his first trip to the cupboard. He wouldn't bring the bottle into the living room, keep it conveniently at his elbow—only a lush worked with a bottle at his side. Bill wasn't a heavy or even a compulsive drinker; at least, he liked to think he wasn't. Nor would he take enough to blur his vision or his speech. He made a point of this.

But three or four times before he came up to bed she would hear his slippered footsteps making for the kitchen. There would be a creak when he opened the refrigerator, a soft plopping as the ice cubes jumped out of the rubber tray, the running of water for a chaser. She could almost hear the tiny cold clink of glass on glass as he filled the tumbler.

He would be sober when he came up, by anyone's test, but a little fuzzy with alcohol and fatigue. It made it easier for her to pretend she was asleep.

She opened her book. It was the story of a young girl, pretty and naïve, who ran away from home because her family and high school sweetheart couldn't accept her being different. In Greenwich Village, perhaps, she could make a life of her own. Frances had opened the door of the rented apartment and timorously explored the rooms with her, had entered the gay bar and hopefully looked at the girls in chinos and car coats. Across the room she caught the eye of a slim beautiful girl—

Tonight she couldn't lose herself in the story. The pleasant, made-up faces of the Wives came between her and the unknown girl.

She read the page over again.

Downstairs there was a rustling as Bill pushed aside his papers and got up for his first trip to the kitchen.

Thank God for liquor, Frances mused. Maybe if I could get really stoned I'd go out and pick up a girl. Just any old girl who would do what Bake used to do in bed.

She had heard of gay girls who went to prostitutes. But she was afraid of disease. She had seen pictures—she shuddered. And besides, she thought angrily, there ought to be a little feeling in it. Even if it's only friendliness.

The last time she had picked up a girl had been the night before Bob's wedding. And what happened? She was raped, beaten up and robbed. Probably wouldn't happen again in a hundred years, but the memory still made her feel sick.

This was unbearable. And it could go on all night.

She pushed down the sheet, seeing in the soft light her still slender and desirable body, so long empty and unfulfilled. It had been so long. You can't count what Bill does to me, she thought coldly. I don't take any real part in it—it doesn't mean any more than what a doctor does when he examines you. There's no shared feeling in it.

In the bathroom she found the little bottle of sedative tablets. Bill took one sometimes, when he was hung over. She swallowed one, capping the bottle tightly and putting it back on the top shelf. She had heard about women who took more and more sleeping pills, forgetting in their drugged condition that they already had some. She didn't really believe she would do anything so stupid, but she wasn't going to take any chances. Anybody was entitled to be silly now and then.

Back in bed she folded the sheet tightly across her chest to give herself a feeling of being held—all right, return to the womb if you feel like it—and lay waiting for sleep. She thought about Bake for a while, although the memory made her more uneasy. And about Kay with her slender taut body and eager mind. And then, at last, she let herself think about Erika Frohmann.

Erika, like sad, tender, faraway music.

She felt her thoughts blur and her head grow heavy as the medication took hold. Her physical desire dissolved into a gentle oblivion. She fell asleep thinking of Erika.

8 THE MEETING, LIKE MOST OF THE MEETINGS FRANces had attended, broke up quickly after the cookies and coffee were served. Vince walked to the door with the speaker, a small dry-voiced man from the American Civil Liberties Union, and some of the others stood around shaking hands and commenting on his talk. "It was certainly kind of you to come, and we'll all remember what you've told us."

"I hope you'll never need to," Mr. Murphy said. "Just keep in mind that you have exactly the same rights as any other citizens—that includes the right to be regarded as innocent until you're proven guilty, and the right to be represented by attorney. If you're ever in a bar having a drink, a place that's licensed to serve liquor, and the police come in and start making arrests, the first thing is to demand legal counsel. The Union will send one if you can't afford the fees."

"What if they ask outright, are you gay?"

"You don't even know what the word means. Keep on insisting that you didn't know what kind of a place it was. Besides, it's not against the law to be gay."

A slender girl with close-cut black curls protested, "That's not honest."

"How can you be honest when you're dealing with a crooked social system?" Vince asked eagerly. "Entrapment is wrong, but they do it all the time." The others nodded.

The speaker shook hands again, put on his hat and left. There was a respectful silence till the sound of his footsteps died away. Then one of the boys—Frances hadn't sorted them out yet—said, "Guess I have to go, I'm working in the morning," and there was a general move to pick up lighters, cigarettes, and leaflets.

Frances stood beside Erika. She said diffidently, not looking at her, "I'm taking a taxi. Can I drop you somewhere?"

"No, I'll wash the cups before I go."

Vince said, "Oh, doll, that's not necessary. I'll do it in the morning."

"No, I'll do it."

"I'll help," Frances said. It would be an excuse to look at Erika for a while, anyway. She began gathering up cups and ashtrays from chair arms, folding trays and the floor. Erika stood a moment looking at her; she was conscious of that clear-eyed gaze but not sure what it meant. She went into the kitchen and stood beside the sink trying to stop her knees from shaking.

Vince shut the apartment door behind the last guest. "How do you like my place?" he asked with boyish eagerness, coming into the kitchen and leaning against the cupboard while Frances scraped and stacked.

"I like it. It's uncluttered."

"I did it myself. Everything's from the shop, or something my grandmother had stashed away in her attic."

The two rooms were what she had expected; she had felt at home here as soon as she stepped inside. Walls painted white, renovated furniture painted dead black, a long bookcase of boards and glass brick not unlike the one Bake had made, a shawl or tapestry in bright colors thrown across the largest chair. The couch was a foam-rubber mattress neatly sewed into a denim cover, resting on a door and four short metal legs. Hinge supports still jutted from the empty doorframes. Somewhere in a closet or drawer, Frances knew, were the sheets that turned this mattress into a bed at night.

She was telling the truth when she said she liked it. Functional, bare, decorated enough by the shelves of books in their colored jackets, it was a free-feeling place. A cheap, unframed Picasso print hung above the kitchenette range. It was such an apartment as she might have furnished for herself, given the freedom.

Vince said, "I wish I had a fireplace, though."

Erika was washing dishes briskly, holding them under the hot tap to rinse and turning them upside down on the drainboard. Under the strong light she looked weary, the lines at the corners of her eyes deepened by fatigue. She had sat in a shaded corner all evening, silent; Frances, acutely aware of her, had turned now and then to look at her, but she hadn't smiled or looked up. The others shifted position, whispered a comment, lit a cigarette, but Erika was immobile. What discipline was this, Frances wondered, to keep her still so long? What was she thinking about?

Now she finished her work, twisted the sink plug and stood waiting while the soapy water gurgled away. Vince unfolded two clean towels and handed one to Frances. "Since you insist."

She worked mechanically, trying to think of some excuse to prolong the evening. Erika would go, still silent—she couldn't bear it. She said hopefully, "It's been an interesting meeting. Thanks for letting me come. Can I buy you both a drink somewhere?" And was at once aware that Vince knew what she was doing. He brushed away a smile with the back of his hand. "I've got some things to do, but maybe Erika would take you up on that."

Erika said formally, "Thank you very much, but I'd like to go home."

Frances was abashed. Vince said, "Look, doll, she isn't asking for your hand in marriage, she just asked you to stop in somewhere for a drink. One drink."

"Why don't you let me alone?"

Now it was between Vince and Erika. Frances didn't even know what the quarrel was about. She realized that Vince was on her side—at least, his interest at this point coincided with hers, which was something—and that she had better keep out of it. She waited. He said crossly, "You have to start living some time. You can't go around like a zombie the rest of your life. Why can't you even act decent to your own kind of people?"

Erika's mouth dropped. "All right, I'll go. I don't care."

Frances's heart thumped. Where can I take her? What will I

say to her when we're alone? She had meant the invitation to be casual, an open-end thing. Now it seemed full of implications. Make a mistake now, she thought, and this girl is out of reach permanently. She felt a scary prickling along her arms.

Erika checked her skirt pockets to be sure her door key was in one, change purse in the other; stood on tiptoe for Vince's goodnight kiss; preceded Frances down the stairs. Vince stood at the door to see them off. At the bottom of the flight, Frances turned back to look at him. He gave her a tremendous wink. She followed Erika out into the night, feeling like a blundering fool. And hungry. Hungry for this girl's touch and the sound of her voice. She felt tired and confused. How was she going to say what she had to say? How could she, who had never approached anyone before, take the initiative?

They stood on the corner waiting for a taxi, so near that Frances could feel the other girl's body warmth, yet each shut into her own thoughts. But in the taxi, with the door shut, Erika came to life. "Do you mind if I go straight home? I'm too tired to be good company. And much too tired to drink," she added with the ghost of a smile.

"Of course. What's the address?"

It meant nothing to her, she didn't know the town. The driver nodded and made an illegal turn in the middle of the block.

Erika sat as she had in Vince's place, hands folded on her knees in the classic posture of resignation. Frances could think of nothing to say. She looked out of the window and wished for this abortive evening to be over.

They slowed in front of a rundown wooden house with cupola, bay windows, and gingerbread porches—an old house, elegant in its day, now scaling and with a "Room To Rent" sign in the front window. Frances found change in her clutch bag and paid the fare. Erika stood on the sidewalk, looking away. Frances leaned out. "It's been nice seeing you again," she said with idiotic punctilio. "I'll see you soon, I hope."

"Do you want to come in for a while?"

Frances stared.

"It's all right if you do."

"Yes, of course."

She stumbled, getting out of the cab. The driver grabbed her arm. His touch broke the unreality that had surrounded her on this dream ride through night streets. Frances stood beside Erika on the sidewalk, afraid to open her mouth because no matter what she said, it was likely to be the wrong thing.

Erika sighed, taking the key from the pocket of her full cotton skirt. "Come in, if you care to. I'll make some coffee."

Did she want Frances to refuse? And if so, why invite her? At any rate, the taxi was gone; she would have to call another before she could leave. Climbing up the two long flights of stairs, watching the worn toe-catching places in the carpeting, hearing her heels clatter on each step, she tried to puzzle it out. It was politeness, she decided, or an unwilling concession to Vince. Not liking—certainly not interest.

The key grated in the lock. Erika smiled, holding the door open. "Come in. I'm sorry I don't have a fan, it gets quite warm sometimes."

The room was very neat and entirely without personality. A door here, two windows there, narrow baseboards and a view of the house next door. It was no wonder she had relented on the invitation, faced with another evening in this barren place. Almost anything would be better than staying alone here, unable to sleep. The room breathed loneliness. Here Erika had slept (surely with the help of tranquilizers, or briefly after long hours of lying awake and remembering); she had risen and scrubbed herself spotless in the chipped tub, had made coffee and gone out to meet another day's teaching. To this room she had returned at four o'clock, carrying an armful of papers to grade. Until summer had come, leaving hours that she had to fill somehow, alone and bereft.

It was no wonder she tended store for Vince.

There was a double bed with a sag in the middle, covered by one of those fancy rayon bedspreads so dear to landladies, a washed-out pink that certainly had nothing to do with Erika Frohmann—unless it was the color of frustration. Without lifting it, Frances knew that it concealed sheets with large press-on patches and a mostly cotton blanket of vaguely Indian design. There was the wooden chest of drawers with the flawed mirror and the one straight chair left over from a 1910 dining room suite. On a small table near the door were the round electric plate, the tin of coffee, percolator washed every morning under the bathroom tap and dried with a piece of Kleenex, a couple of plastic cups. Erika picked up the pot and stood looking at it vaguely, as though wondering what to do with it. Catching Frances's eye, she smiled politely. "Why don't you sit down? I'll make some coffee."

"Thanks."

Erika left, carrying the aluminum pot carefully, as though it might shatter in her hand. Frances sat on the edge of the bed facing the second door, behind which, no doubt, Erika kept her clothes.

"I'm sorry, I haven't any cream," Erika apologized, looking less nervous now that she had something to do.

"I take it black."

"So do I."

The wires of the hot plate glowed dull, then bright. Erika measured the grounds carefully, adjusted the little glass hat to tighten it, and set the whole contraption on the heat. Frances said, to break the silence, "I hope I'm not making too much bother for you."

"No—oh no, only I wish Vince would mind his own business. Always trying to help other people's troubles. Things will work out without help—and if they don't, what can he do about it? Nothing, that's all."

Frances said, "I'm not trying to intrude." And knew she was lying.

"I suppose he had to tell you about Kate and me."

"A little."

Erika's smile was drawn. "Vince is so young. Twenty-seven, but he still thinks all sorrows can be cured. Or that love is the answer to everything. What does he know about love?"

Frances said heavily, "I don't think one person ever takes the places of another. But sometimes a new person can make a place of her own."

"It's not the same."

Oh God, Frances prayed, don't let me give up hope, don't make it hopeless when I could love her so dearly. She sat looking at the closet door, knowing there was no right answer. Erika said, "Vince thinks all I need is to go to bed with someone. I tried that."

"It didn't work?"

"No. It was sickening. I don't have those feelings anymore."

The coffee began to make happy noises. Erika turns the switch down to *M* for medium. The wire coils dulled and the sound diminished. She said stiffly. "I also tried getting drunk first. That's no good either."

"It takes time," Frances said tritely.

"I'm almost thirty. Oh God," Erika said, her voice breaking, "I may live to be a hundred. What am I supposed to do?"

Frances said in a smothered voice, "It matters to me. Do you think it doesn't matter?"

There was deep sadness in Erika's face. "I can't understand it. I was always the strong one, always. Kate was sick when she came to me. She was an alcoholic—she was really sick. I made her well."

"Well, I'm not Kate, and things have changed for you too."

"Some people think that all the body cells change every seven years, and we become different people," Erika said with a melancholy attempt at humor. "Do you believe that?"

France's heart was banging. She got to her feet. Erika sat with her head down, refusing to acknowledge her approach. She put a shaking hand on Erika's shoulder. The bone was flint hard under a too thin covering of flesh. Erika sat unmoving under her hand, like a captive bird. Only the front of her cotton shirt rose unevenly.

"I love you," Frances said. The statement sounded cold and flat. "You know that, don't you?"

"I know it."

"I'm serious about it."

"I know that too. I'm sorry."

She moved from under Frances's hand and turned off the hot plate. The coffee was done.

Frances stood motionless, shocked and frightened. Now I've done it. Now I've spoiled everything.

Erika handed her a plastic cup, wisps of steam rising from it. "Don't be unhappy," she said gently. "Drink your coffee; then you will want to go. It's getting late."

"Of course."

The coffee was bitter. They sat enclosed in their separate miseries, afraid to look at each other. Frances found it hard to swallow. When the two cups were empty, Erika stood up. She moved a little stiffly, as though deeply tired, but her mouth smiled. She touched Frances's hand lightly. "I like you," she said apologetically. "Please don't be sorry. I like you very much. It's only that love frightens me." Erika shut her eyes. "It's not your fault. Give me a little time. Maybe we could be friends. I'd like to have you for a friend."

"Can I kiss you goodnight?"

"If you want to." But her voice was dull, and she kept her face half turned away. Frances was afraid to kiss her on the mouth. She touched her lips quickly to Erika's check, which was cool and impassive.

She stood at the door of her room, frowning in a troubled way, while Frances went softly down the stairs and let herself out into the late night. The air was soft and dark with summer. A thousand scents rose from the grass and flowering bushes. Looking up, Frances saw Erika reach up and close the window, shutting out the heat and the sweetness.

9 "I DON'T KNOW WHAT'S THE MATTER WITH YOU." Bill was trying to be calm, but his voice shook, always a sign that he was about to lose his temper. A thousand sales meetings and ten thousand customer contacts had taught him to be nasty in a controlled way, Frances supposed.

She stood beside the bookcase wishing he would shut up. She sighed.

"I know it takes a while to get used to a new town, this place is pretty small and everything, but Jesus Christ, you never did anything so goddamn wonderful in Chicago as far as I could see. Except take some courses at the university and sit around in that lousy insurance office, working for peanuts while your home went to pieces."

Frances managed to keep her mouth shut. She looked past him, focusing on the maple tree in the side yard. As though cut from bright green paper, the many-pointed leaves moved slightly in the evening breeze. Think about leaves, how green and cool they are.

"I'm doing everything I can to make you happy. I don't make any fuss about all these rugs and tables and stuff you're always buying. Oh no, I'm good enough to pay the bills, the way you buy stuff anybody would think money grew on trees, but you don't catch me complaining. I'm proud to give you a nice home, anything you want, it's okay by me—"

"Oh, Bill."

Conciliatory, wifelike—and useless. She bit back other words, knowing what every married woman learns early in her marriage, that there's no point in reasoning with a frustrated man. He doesn't want reason; it's the reasonableness of things that makes him angry. He wants reassurance and praise, the little woman act, the buildup.

"You can't complain that my friends aren't nice to you, either." Now he was off on some tangent of his own, no use trying to figure where his thought processes were leading him. Whatever had led to this outburst must have been rankling for quite a while. "They've been damn nice to you, all because you're my wife. Pete Prendergast says Betty asked you to join some card club the girls have and you told her you were too busy. Doing what, or shouldn't I ask? What are you doing that's more important than making friends?"

"Oh, Bill, they get all dressed up like plush horses, and they fix fancy refreshments and sit around and gossip. I went once. I don't like poker anyhow."

"That's because you're a lousy player. You'd be all right if you kept your mind on the game."

"It seems like such a waste of time. Anyway, I had a party for your friends. Besides having the Wives to lunch."

"I suppose my friends' wives aren't good enough for you to associate with. You'd sooner hang around with a bunch of freaks in pants and have decent people laughing at you."

People with double chins shouldn't lose their tempers, Frances thought. But she felt a flash of indignation. A series of faces passed in gentle review between her eyes and the cut-leaf maple. Bake, with a preoccupied frown between her thick, dark eyebrows; Kay's shining eyes and lovely sensitive mouth; Erika, sad and austere. My own people, she thought, intelligent and brave in a world that rejects them. This man with the red, angry face was the enemy.

Bill said in complete exasperation, "You could at least say something. You don't have to be so damn snotty."

"Am I?"

"You could answer when I'm talking to you."

"What do you want me to say?"

He clenched his fist. For a panicky moment she thought he was going to hit her. It took all the courage she had not to duck. Then his hand dropped and he stood frowning at her. "Francie, why do you act like this? Anybody'd think you were doing it on purpose."

All right, she would give it one last try. She said, choosing her words with care and hoping he might possibly, just possibly get it, "I'm a person, not just a wife. I have to figure things out for myself and decide what I want to do with my life—what's left of it."

He said brightly, "Hell, you haven't got any problem. It's all worked out for you. There isn't a nicer bunch of fellows anywhere than the men at the office, and their wives all like you. I'm making good money. You can have anything you want, within reason. You're a nice-looking woman, bright, and it's a hell of a lot easier to be somebody in a town like this than it is in a big city. My good God, the whole set-up is made to order for you."

What can you say, what arguments can you possibly use in the face of new furniture and three charge accounts?

"What do you want, anyhow?"

Love, she thought. Beyond the window, a soft haze was creeping over the maple tree, the shadow of the summer evening. She tried it. She said, swallowing hard, "Love."

"Well, hell, you know I love you. I wouldn't work the way I do if I didn't. My job's no picnic, you know. All the responsibility falls on me. The guys on the assembly line go home at five and leave their job there, but I've got the whole damn thing on my mind all the time." He looked at her, baffled. "Hell, if I didn't love you I wouldn't have taken you back when you got yourself beat up and everything. It wouldn't have been so bad if it was a man—but getting mixed up with those crazy she-males, not many husbands would've put up with that!"

There it was. I've been forgiven at least three hundred times before, she calculated, and even times before, she calculated, and every time I get smaller and he gets bigger. Pretty soon he'll be God Almighty and I won't even exist.

"You don't act like you are interested in love, I'll say that much for you. Every time I lay a hand on you, you start acting like some virgin who's afraid of being raped."

But of course, she thought, that's what sex without love is. It could be an act of friendship, it doesn't have to be the one great passion of a lifetime, but at least it ought to have a little recognition of the other person in it. Nothing to do with a license or a church ceremony; going to bed with somebody you don't care about is just plain wrong. She said coldly, "I'll be glad to divorce you, if that's what you want."

His reaction was one of surprise. His mouth fell open and a dull red crept up his neck and spread over his face. He said, "You're crazy. What do you want a divorce for?"

"You don't seem to be very happy."

"That's what I'm trying to get across to you, for God's sake. Why can't you try to do better?"

Frances was silent.

The old lady next door came out of her house, perky in a white hat like a pie plate, a huge white bag swinging from her shriveled arm, and took off on some evening errand of her own. As though the sight of another human being had released her from her trance, Frances took a step backward. "I'm going out."

"What for? It's almost bedtime."

"It's twenty minutes after eight."

"You're not safe alone on the streets after dark."

"This isn't Chicago, and anyhow it won't be dark for another hour. I don't feel particularly safe here, listening to you yell."

Her keys lay on the hall table, a little bunch of glitter. She dropped them into her pocket and stepped outside. Let him sulk alone if he feels like sulking.

She almost wished he would do something violent, like beating her, or locking her out, or leaving. Anything would be better than listening to this for the next thirty or forty years. Well then, resolve it. Become one of the Wives. It probably hadn't come natural to some of them; some of them had gone to college. They must suspect that there was more to life than having their hair done. If they could learn, she could.

For what? Another thirty years of boredom, and retirement to Florida with a dull old man at the end?

The neighborhood was quiet, a few cars on the street, a few couples walking, housewives sitting on their screened front porches. A thin young man in bermudas stood at the curb, lovingly polishing a small foreign car. He glanced at Frances and went back to his polishing. She smiled. Five years ago, the automatic rejection would have stung. Now she walked on, wondering what his girl was like—he wasn't married, that was a bachelor's car, and how she felt about getting married. Probably crazy to. They all wanted to catch a man at seventeen and have four babies in rapid succession these days.

She walked briskly past comfortable two-story houses much like her own (or Bill's), some modernized with iron scrollwork and stylized shutters, some old-fashioned and homey. Her irritation with Bill was beginning to evaporate, leaving a residue of pity. Poor guy, he had a real grievance. All he wanted was a wife like everybody else's wife. He had been as kind as he knew how to be. It was the kindness that wore her down, like paying interest on a debt year after year and never making a dent on the principal. Forty years from now he would still be nobly forgiving her for the only whole-hearted relationship she had ever known.

She wished that just once she could hate somebody without any mental reservations. It would be a pleasure. She wished she didn't feel sorry for him.

It had been a mistake, naturally, to tell him how she felt. They couldn't communicate. They could talk about trifles like the blanket she had just bought for Mari's baby, and marvel over the wonders of Dacron. But when it came to feelings they were like a cat and a parakeet in the same household, the mewing of the one and the chirping of the other making no sense.

An elderly man came toward her with two dachshunds on leashes. She bent to admire the dogs, and the man gave her a sour look. She hurried on. Let's be fair, she admonished herself, teetering on a curb to let a car go by. Nobody really understands anybody else. Even Bake—I never did know why she drank so much, what was in her past that made her need to, or why she got those desperate moods. She probably didn't know herself. Or Bob. People are always telling you how they understand their kids, but I never really knew what was going on in Bob's head; it was a relief to have Mari take over.

It was really getting dark. The houses were shadowy; windows glowed from within. Frances began to feel a little uneasy. Her feet ached. And for all her coolness, she was a little afraid to be out alone after dark. It seemed unlikely that crime was confined to big cities; even in this quiet suburban town the paper reported purse snatchings and knifings.

She didn't want to go back to the house on Regent Street. If Bill were still being righteously angry she would be in for more of the same thing. If he's simmered down and taken a drink or two he was likely to start pawing. She didn't know which was worse.

A cab came around the corner and pulled to a stop just ahead of her. A slender young girl got out and stood waiting while her escort paid the driver. Frances moved quickly. "Are you free?"

"Sure am. Where you wanta go?"

She had heard Erika's address only once, but it came to her lips as though it was her own. The driver, an intelligent-looking young Negro, pushed back his cap. "You're a long ways from home. That's way over on the other side of town."

"It's a nice night for a ride."

No money. If she isn't there I can't pay. What do they do, put you in jail? Mail it to him later, or there's Vince, I can call him up. She got into the cab, trying to look calm.

Way across town wasn't far for someone used to big city distances. There was the house, gaunt and falling apart. The driver settled back and waited while she ran up the front steps. The outer door was unlocked, probably didn't even have a lock. There was no one in the dim downstairs hall. Mail lay on a small table beside a telephone. She climbed the two flights of stairs and stood a moment, irresolute, in front of Erika's door. Light shone through the transom. She knocked.

Erika opened the door a crack and looked out, then opened it wider. She had on faded blue cotton pajamas and looked sleepy, although it was still early.

Frances said, "Have you got any money? There's a taxi driver down there waiting to be paid."

"Just a minute." She found a shabby clutch bag in a drawer, dumped its contents out on the bed. Frances held out her hand, but Erika ignored it. She selected a dollar bill, pulled on a terry robe and walked down alone, holding herself erect and looking straight ahead. It was impossible to tell what she was thinking.

She hates me, Frances thought. She'll make me go back. But from the window she saw Erika pay the driver, saw the taxi pull away and roll down the street. She wondered, without really caring, how she was going to get home. When Erika came in, pulling the door shut behind her, she said in a low voice, "I had to come."

"I know." Erika laid a small cool hand on her wrist. It rested there lightly. "I wondered when you were coming."

"Did you want me to?"

"I don't know." A small smile changed the shape of Erika's mouth, making her look both younger and sadder. "As long as you're here, why don't you sit down?"

She slid the bolt in the door.

10

WITHOUT THE COTTON PAJAMAS, ERIKA WAS slight and small, like a child. Below the collarbone her skin was milky white, the little breasts those of an adolescent, the nipples tight and hard as unopened buds. Frances ran a gentle hand down over the flat belly, to the secret triangle of curling reddish hair. "Tell me if you want me to stop," she said softly.

"I don't want you to stop," Erika whispered. Under the glaring light her face was shut and expressionless. But when Frances bent to kiss her, she opened her mouth slightly. "Turn off the light, it hurts."

Frances was filled to overflowing with love. Let me make her happy, she prayed silently. Nothing else was important. Only joy and fulfillment for Erika, who needed so badly to be made happy. She moved to set her lips against a little pink bud.

Much later, she lay awake in the moonlight, feeling the gentle rise and fall of Erika's breathing. The rest of the world was far away, safely shut out. She had no way of knowing how much time passed before Erika moved. "Frances?"

"Are you awake?"

"Mm."

"Sorry?"

Erika sat up in bed, groping for the wall's switch. The ceiling light flashed on clear and bright. Frances put an arm around Erika's shoulders and drew her close, half afraid of being rebuffed. "Are you happy?"

Erika took the question seriously. "I don't know. Let me get up." She pulled away to reach for her terry robe. With the belt knotted around her waist she seemed again the remote girl Frances had been uselessly wanting. She said slowly, "It's different."

"From—her?"

"No, I mean I'm different." The wrinkle between her eyes deepened, but she managed a smile. She sat down on the bed, of her own accord leaning against Frances, as though the contact comforted her. "You know, twice in my life I had to give up hope. In the camp where all those soldiers did bad things to me, when I was only twelve years old. That's too young for so much badness. So I decided never to let anyone touch me again."

"I'm sorry."

"Only with men. I don't hate men the way some gay girls do, you know how much I love Vince—it's only that I don't like to make love with them. After the accident I decided all over again, no love." Erika looked under the bed and dredged up a pair of shabby ballet slippers. She sat with them in her hands. "How can anyone resign from the human race? Now you brought me back to life. I don't know whether to hate you or say thank you."

"I don't want to hurt you. Or make you sad."

She rested her head against Frances's bare shoulder. "I won't ever lie to you. I wanted you. When you were here the other night, after the meeting, I wanted you so badly it frightened me."

"That's why you sent me home, then. I thought you were angry at me for bothering you."

"I was angry at myself. Because I have this feeling about you," Erika said slowly, "I don't want to call it anything, but I do know I don't want to get mixed up with anyone again. I want to stay frozen."

Frances said smiling, "You didn't act frozen."

Erika looked ashamed. "The body. It says do this, do that, and you have no choice. It's like Pavlov's dogs, someone rings the little bell and the body reacts. I don't want to hurt you, but that's not love."

"It's a part of love," Frances said stubbornly. "It can be the beginning. At least you don't hate me, do you?"

"I'm attracted to you." Erika's best smile flashed out. "Do you think I'd let you in my room if you were only a trick? Sooner I'd stay alone all my life. Also, I trust you."

Frances said in a hurt voice, "That's something."

"How about you? Do you love someone?"

"Not anymore. Not unless it's you."

"Maybe you should get up and go away now. I'd like to have you stay forever, but that's being sentimental. Also there are things I have to think about."

"Yes, of course." Frances looked at the cheap alarm clock on the dresser. It was almost two. She said uneasily, "I don't have any money. I didn't plan to come here—I went for a walk, and suddenly I had to see you."

"I have some." Erika unzipped the clutch bag and emptied its contents on the sleazy pink spread. A penny rolled to the floor. Comb, lipstick, a couple of dollar bills and some change, a little notebook—that was all. It was the bag of a woman without vanity and with few distractions, who had stripped her life bare of trivial things. It frightened Frances, who took the bill Erika handed her, then put it down again. "I'll pay you back when I see you. When can I see you?"

"When you want to. Call the store, Vince always knows. There is a telephone here, but unless somebody happens to be in the hall, no one answers. Besides, the landlady listens. But I see Vince often."

"You think a lot of him, don't you?"

"I love him. I wish I could find someone for him to love, someone good and kind. He deserves to be happy."

Frances got out of bed, unwilling to leave the warmth of Erika's body and the light scent of her clean hair. Her clothes lay neatly folded over the back of a chair, where Erika had put them. She remembered how she and Bake had dropped their things to the floor, how she and Bake had never need to look away from each other and busy their hands while they gathered courage. None of this tentative touching, this searching of faces in the harsh light to gauge the other's willingness. Bake loved me, Frances thought forlornly. This girl will probably hate me as soon as I'm out of sight.

Already sorry she let me stay, probably.

"What are you thinking about with your face so serious?"

"How nice you are."

Erika's smile was that of a kind mother who takes her hands out of the dishpan to accept a bunch of dandelions. "Don't make me compliments. It's not necessary."

"I mean it." And suddenly it was true. Misgivings, frustrations and all, she felt relaxed and happy for the first time in months. The body, she reminded herself, trying to capture Erika's light scorn as she pulled on her panties and reached behind to hook her bra. Do this, do that, and the fulfilled body moves and purrs like a stroked kitten. But she was unable to minimize it. Even her skin felt good.

She put on her skirt and zipped it up, tucked in her blouse and found her soft brown loafers under the bed where they were lying sociably side by side with Erika's Capezios. From the mirror an awakened face smiled back at her. She remembered, sharply, the first time she had turned to Bake's dressing table after love, the new beauty that shone out of her. A sharp pang thrust her through. Never, never again, no matter who came into her life from this time on. There can only be one first love.

Erika said, "You're thinking about someone."

"Not really."

"Try not to. That's not jealousy; if it made you happy to remember I would be glad for you. When I find Kate's name in a book or someone says it—ah, it's no good." Tears came to Erika's eyes. She turned her face away. "I can't breathe. Maybe it goes away some time, I hope so, because on these terms who can live?"

"I envy the boys. They never seem to get involved the way we do, they just go from person to person. It must be easier."

"Yes. Only sometimes it matters more than they admit. And I have to tell you, Frances, you matter to me. I'm not going from person to person. I have to say this."

"I know."

They kissed briefly, like friends. Erika picked up the dollar and held it out to her. "The telephone is at the foot of the stairs, on a table, and the cab number is written on the wall. I don't know who wrote it there. Try not to wake Mrs. Agnoff," she said, but smiling as though it didn't matter. "If you were a man it would shock her to see you leave so late, but this, I don't think she knows about it." Her smile wavered. "Do you hate me? Will you call me, or come back again?"

"Of course I will."

"Don't let me say no to you. I get scared, but I do truly like you very much."

Well, Frances thought dryly, that's something. She waved goodbye from the bedroom door and tiptoed downstairs, stopping every time a step creaked. No one else seemed to be awake. She found the telephone and the cab company's number (scrawled on dirty plaster) and dialed the number.

A door opened two inches. A metal curler caught the light. "Is anything the matter?"

She smothered a giggle. "No, I'm just calling a cab."

"Well, wait outside. You don't have to wake everybody up."

She stood on the long porch, looking around. The town was still. A single car passed, then another; then a cluster of young girls in party dresses, talking in low voices. Here and there a lighted window framed groups playing cards or the unearthly glow of a television screen.

It would be nice, she thought, to spend a whole night with someone she loved, curled up together with the rest of the world shut out. The thought brought back an unwelcome thought of Bake asleep, her face drowned in moonlight from the open window, her warm solid body fitted against Frances as though even in sleep she couldn't bear for them to be apart. Bake, that was all she knew of woman's tenderness. And Bill? She grimaced.

She had been touched and a little frightened by Erika's thinness, her white skin and the delicacy of her bones. She looked like a boy just entering adolescence, but in bed she was heartshakingly feminine: small shoulders, the slightest of breasts, a body whittled down to bare bone and muscle. Little bird bones, Frances thought tenderly. And now her own body remembered sharply not only the fragility of Erika's body but the intensity with which Erika moved when she aroused to love.

She had never seen the outside of her own house this late at night. It looked strange, all its bulk massed differently. The downstairs windows were lit. She paid the driver and walked slowly up the walk while he waited to make sure she got safely inside.

The door was unlocked. She walked in coolly, dangling her keychain from a finger. Bill was up, still dressed, sitting in a chair reading *US News and World Report*. He looked relieved, then annoyed, then sulky. She turned her face away from him, remembering the alive warmth Erika's mirror had reflected. "I went to the late show and took a taxi home."

"Why didn't you call?"

"Why should I? I figured you were asleep."

"Well I'm not. I'd have come after you."

This was alarming. She had expected—almost hoped for—a renewal of the quarrel. Now she saw that his expression was fatuous. He was waiting up for her, not because he was angry or anxious, but because the desire he resented but couldn't control had taken hold of him again. She had seen it happen before, after a quarrel. He was in the mood for making love.

I can't bear to have him touch me tonight, she thought. Tomorrow if I have to, all right, but not tonight. She said coldly, hating herself—why do women lie with such ease?—"I have a headache. I'm going to take a sedative and go right to sleep."

"Maybe you'd feel better if you took an aspirin. Or an Alka-Seltzer." He closed his magazine and laid it on the table. "How about a drink? Let's both have one."

"Thanks, all I want is to sleep. I'm dead."

He stood there, uncertain. She went quickly upstairs.

She had told herself a dozen times that intercourse was a chore, like washing dishes. Nothing you would choose if you had a choice, but no more than bothersome. If she felt guilty about this, she was also upheld by the knowledge that countless other wives felt the same way. For all the books and magazine articles that were supposed to teach you how to be happy in marriage, all the feeling of security that was supposed to come from being able to regulate conception, she knew from office gossip and books that many women felt nothing at all, or were wakeful and dissatisfied after love. It had nothing to do with loving men or loving women; it was universal.

But at some time during this night she had crossed the line that divides indifference from revulsion. I can't bear it, she thought wildly. I can't let him touch me. (Swallowing her little pill and drinking half a glass of tepid water, frowning.) Maybe later I can figure out the answer. Not tonight.

She got into bed and pulled the sheet right up to her chin, although it was a sultry night and Bill had forgotten to turn on the air-conditioner. Closing her eyes, she tries to recall every detail of the time she spent in Erika's bed.

It was incredible, it was crazy, but in the excitement she had forgotten Bill. He might never have existed, so completely had he dropped out of her mind from the moment she tapped on Erika's door until she reentered her own house. There might have been nothing between Erika and herself except the sweet hurting memory of two other women, one dead, one engrossed in a new love.

How could I? She asked herself, stricken. And knew the answer. Bill didn't matter anymore, except as an obstacle.

The pill was beginning to blur her thoughts. She gave in to it gratefully. Her mind shifted from image to image, without continuity.

I might love her, she thought solemnly. Anyway it's a reasonable facsimile. She might even love me, give her time. It's too complicated. She pressed her hands against her breasts. They felt full and sensitive. The nipples rose full and hard under her fingers. On her arm a dark spot showed, a bruise of love. She smiled, remembering. She heard Bill come to the foot of the stairs. The house was quiet. After a moment he went into the kitchen and opened the cupboard door.

Poor guy, she thought, trying to open her eyes and finding the lids too heavy. She turned over and went to sleep.

11

"THE CHIEF VALUE OF SUCH AN INTERVIEW OR series of interviews," the family relations editor of *Our Home* explained in ten-point italic, "is that it gives each of the marital partners an opportunity to discuss his or her problem with a sympathetic but impartial listener. Thus, the rejected wife in our case history was able to explain her frustrations to a trained counselor who could evaluate her problem from a rational standpoint. By making a real effort to understand the factors that led to their estrangement, both Joe and Sandra developed a clearer understanding of their relationship and a deeper appreciation of their marriage partner. Their marriage is now rated as 'highly successful,' and the case records are closed."

Sounds easy, Frances thought, lifting a shaky hand to ring the doorbell and finding herself unable to do so. At two in the morning, trying to get her mind off Bill's fumbling lovemaking, she had followed the problems of Joe and Sandra with interest—especially the part about discussing the problems with a sympathetic pastor if trained counseling was not available. She certainly couldn't discuss them with the Wives! And Bill's viewpoint was so reasonable as to rule out argument: a man has a right to go to bed with his own wife. So far, she hadn't found any counterargument.

She suspected that Joe and Sandra were of a piece with the other contents of *Our Home*: the saccharine stories of your married love in the higher-priced suburbs, the Technicolor recipes, the advice on how to buy a new electric ironer. Somebody makes the whole thing up, she told herself, looking fixedly at the well-polished brass plate that said "Dr. Daniel S. Powell, Rector." She rang the bell.

Her knees were rubbery, her mouth dry, but as long as she was here she was going through with it. Maybe he would be out.

The door opened. A thin, youngish man in paint-spotted work clothes smiled at her. "Come on in. I'm making coffee."

At least he didn't have the unctuous look of young preachers. Been at it long enough to relax, maybe. She said shakily, "Maybe I shouldn't have called. I'm not a member of your church."

"Then I won't have to treat you like one," Dr. Powell said pleasantly. "Why don't you come in and have coffee, anyway?" He led the way into a long, light room, stopping to pat a fluffy cat lying in a rocking chair. "I don't know why anyone goes to a minister for advice, anyway. We don't know more than other people, and we have an unhappy tendency to be sanctimonious."

Frances laughed. "It's cheaper than going to an analyst, and not as painful as shock treatment. They wouldn't come if you charged twenty dollars an hour."

"I don't mind. It's the masochist in me." His voice was cheerful, but he had a melancholy face; American Gothic, and he was older than she had thought at first. And where was Mrs. Powell? Anyway, she thought, he's safe with me. Is he ever safe with me!

"Do you like kitchens? I can bring our coffee into the living room if you like, but I have a pretty good kitchen and it's handy for refills."

It was a good kitchen, with a teeming Breughel print tacked up over the sink and a spreading maple tree beyond the windows. A pleasant clutter prevailed. "Whoever does your housework has a nice place for it," she told him, and caught the amused gleam in his eyes. "I do my own housework, except for a lady who comes in two mornings a week to pick up after me. I think I'm pretty handy, but she doesn't seem to think so—but then, she's Pennsylvania Dutch." He offered cream and sugar in bright pottery, but seemed pleased when she refused both. "I take mine black too. It has more wallop that way."

"Hot coffee's the best thing on a summer day."

"Would you like a drink? I have some good Irish whiskey."

"This is fine."

He sat down on a high stool, swinging a foot. There was

paint on his moccasins too. He said, "I've been painting the upstairs study and working out an exchange plan for preachers—let everybody go to a stranger for advice and then attend Sunday services in his own church. Or vice versa. That way, people can keep their own pastors thinking well of them. They always feel they have to put their best foot forward with the minister, and it's an awful drag."

"I don't go to church at all."

"I wouldn't either if I didn't have to. It's pretty hard to listen to most sermons and retain any faith in God, even if the sermons are kept down to twenty minutes." He eyed her over the rim of his cup. "How did you pick me, from the phone book?"

"I liked the looks for your church. The old ones mostly look like something out of the Middle Ages and the new ones are all plastic and anodized aluminum." She hesitated. "Then I was going by one day and you were out talking to a crabby-looking old woman. She was yelling at five or six little kids for playing on the church steps, and you came out and gave her hell. I mean—"

Dan Powell's lips quirked. "If you could just forget I'm a preacher and pretend I'm a human being, maybe you could tell me what's bothering you. I don't have any magic for solving problems, you know. Why don't you just mutter an incantation and turn me into a friend?"

"Well, if you're not married—"

"I do know the facts of life. I've even read Kinsey. And Reich. I think they both underestimate the role of emotion, but I guess their findings are fairly accurate."

"Well." She looked at him. He sounded all right, but this wasn't one of those usual problems like being in love with another man or not wanting a baby or having an unfaithful husband. He would probably think it was a neurosis. They were always harping on that: retarded development, parental rejection, childhood trauma, inherited tendency. As if straight people didn't have all the same things to cope with.

Maybe she could make up something plausible. She didn't look butch.

"What's the matter, don't you know where to begin? Tell me something about yourself. Anything. Any birthmarks? Allergies?"

She took a deep breath. "Well, I'm almost forty and I've been married since I was nineteen. My husband is manager of a plastics factory—I hate plastics too. I have a son, nineteen, who's a freshman at Urbana. He's married and they expect a baby in February."

She stopped, aghast at the picture she was drawing. This was Mrs. William Ollenfield with her seams straight and her hair freshly set. She said, "I'm not like that at all."

"I don't believe you are. Do you work? Do you do something you're interested in?"

"No. I had an office job for a while, but it was just a way to get out of the house. Most jobs are."

Dr. Powell said, "Why don't you pretend I'm a reporter for *Confidential* and you're being interviewed?"

"You look more like an explorer. Not that I know what explorers look like."

He laughed. "I look like a man who's painting the upstairs study. Go ahead. Who've you killed?"

She said desperately, "I'm a lesbian."

"What am I supposed to do, drop dead?"

She stared. He said, "Every tenth woman in the United States is a homosexual. Every sixth man. Always happens when you get a civilization growing rapidly decadent. You've got a lot of company."

"You're not shocked?"

"I've known about it since I was maybe fourteen. I can see how you might be upset if you just found out, of course."

"No. It's been quite a while."

"Doing anything about it?"

"You mean therapy?"

"No, that's not what I mean."

"Oh. Well, I'm not sure, things are a little confused right now. I have hopes, you might say." She stared at him. "Doesn't your seminary tell you what to do in cases like this?"

Dr. Powell smiled, "I think I'm supposed to recommend that twenty-dollar analyst." He fitted his fingertips together and adjusted imaginary glasses. "With therapy, Mrs. Ollenfield, you can be restored to a useful role in society."

It was so exactly what she had expected that she couldn't help laughing. She said, "It isn't funny, though."

"It certainly isn't. I hope you've loved someone very much."

"Yes. The girl who brought me out."

"What happened?"

What *had* happened? Bake's drinking, Bake's tempers because she wouldn't divorce Bill and move into the apartment, Bake's betrayal of her with Jane, were these the causes of their split? Or was it her own cowardice that kept her from taking the final step? It was too complicated. There were too many factors to weigh, and she didn't know how.

She fastened on the most obvious cause. "My son was engaged to a girl from a very conservative family. He asked me to give up my friend. Some messy things happened and they both knew about it—my husband and my son." She shivered, remembering the awful night with a girl who beat her and raped her and left her to get home, bruised and penniless, in time for Bob's wedding. It was too awful to tell anyone, even this thin man with the kind eyes.

She said hastily, "Then my husband forgave me and took me back. He's gone on forgiving me for more than a year now, and I don't think I can stand much more of it."

"He doesn't love you."

"He thinks he does."

"If he loved you the way any human being needs to be loved, one act of forgiveness would be enough—and he'd ask you to forgive him."

"What for?"

"How do I know? You don't love him either, do you?"

"Sometimes I hate him." To admit it was a relief. She said, "I keep trying to tell him how I feel, but he won't listen. He seems to think it's my own fault if I'm not satisfied. He earns good money—he gives me things I don't want—"

"Do you sleep with him? Don't tell me if you don't want to."

"Twice a week, on schedule." Her voice was bitter. She didn't mean it to be, but it was. "I feel like a prostitute."

"And—you're with someone else too? Some girl?"

"Only once. I don't know how it's going to work out, but I want her if she'll have me." She looked at him, at his thin listening face above the open-neck shirt. "Don't tell me I'm abnormal. I feel normal with Erika, but not with Bill."

"Would your husband want to go on living with you if he knew about her?"

"I don't know. Before, he seemed to think it was just a phase, like being mentally ill for a while. I did something that upset him, and now it's over." She ran her tongue over dry lips. "It's nice like that. Everything that's decent and honest is tied up with it. I'm not casual." She said defensively, "I'm not talking just about sex, there's love in it."

"There is indeed," Dr. Powell said, sounding unhappy. "What would happen if you left him?"

"I can type and file and take dictation. I could earn a living."

"Then why are you asking me? You really have it all worked out in your own mind."

Frances set her cup down hard. The coffee splashed. She said, "I didn't know I had. I guess I wanted some kind of an okay—you know? It's easy to know what to do, but doing it is something else. Maybe I'm not brave enough."

"You have to find your own courage."

"I don't want to hurt Bill."

He shook his head. "You can't help it. Nobody lives without hurting other people. You simply have to decide how to do the least possible harm—what's right for you is often right for others too. You're going to hurt Bill if you keep on living in the same house, pulling away from him. You've hurt him already."

Frances sighed. She stood up. "Well—thanks, Dr. Powell."

"People who like me generally call me Dan."

"I'm Frances. Anyway, thanks a lot. Especially," she said, moving ahead of him into the living room and look absently at a row of Toby jugs on the mantel, "for not thinking I'm a case of retarded development or something. Straight people almost never realize that what seems abnormal to them might be perfectly normal for somebody else."

Dan Powell said seriously, "Frances, there aren't any rules. Try not to hurt anybody—but remember, it's better to inflict a small hurt now than a big one later on. No one can tell you what to do." He laid a brotherly hand on her shoulder. "Come again. Who knows, we might find we're friends."

She went away quietly.

Something had been decided. She would have laughed at the idea that a total stranger could make up her mind for her—and yet, she thought, I only needed someone to tell me what I knew all along. Someone I could respect.

Nothing was changed, but she went home full of new hope.

12 IT WAS DISHEARTENING, WHEN SHE REACHED the house of Regent Street, to find Bill out and a note on the refrigerator door. Visiting firemen—don't wait up. She went to bed, rehearsing what she would say when she had a chance.

I appreciate your kindness, but our marriage is a failure and it's not fair to either of us to go on like this. Then what? He might hit her—but no, he was the kind of man who calls in a lawyer and signs papers. Anyway, she was going to tell him the truth. All except, maybe, the visit to Dan Powell (and what a pastoral consultation that had been, she thought grinning; the editors of *Our Home* should only know).

She fell asleep thinking how easy it is to evade a lover when you don't feel like seeing him, but husbands—they were always under foot when you didn't want them; you were tied to them by hoops of steel: the double bed, the breakfast table, the joint checking account. And if you wanted fifteen minutes alone with the man to whom you were bound, he had a sales meeting.

She woke to a day streaming with sunshine. Bill was already dressed and shaved. "I'll eat at the drugstore. You were sleeping so sound I hated to wake you." He yawned. "Christ, what a night. Schubert and I are taking these three wops to Chicago tonight, last night they're here. Expect me when you see me."

"Wops?"

"They're opening a branch plastics factory in Venice. Here to study American business methods."

Venice. City of the Doges and the Bridge of Sighs, newly dedicated to pink plastic blocks and aqua cereal dishes. She said drowsily, "I should have gone to Europe sooner. Too late."

"Huh?"

"Do they drink Coca-Cola in Venice?"

"Hell, how would I know?"

When he was gone she jumped out of bed and dressed, her heartbeat accelerating. It was going to be a scorcher, the kind of weather where you could actually hear corn growing. Sunshine poured in at the open windows. The house was full of that hot, still, leisurely feeling that goes with summer in a small city. It was the kind of day she liked best, a day that filled her with strong, hot energy.

Bake had liked cold winds and walks in the snow. She didn't know yet what Erika liked. She didn't know much about Erika, except the way she broke into passionate flame when her body was aroused. It was all to be learned.

She had been separated from Erika—she looked at the wall clock—thirty-three hours. It was too long. Already, she was hungry for the sight of Erika's face and the touch of her hand. And how did Erika feel by this time? Was she happy, or sorry that the shell of her loneliness had been broken? Frances couldn't wait to find out.

She dropped her keys into a skirt pocket and stepped out into the bright clear sunshine. Two boys stood at the bus stop, their hands touching. She smiled at them, then turned away to give them a little privacy while she waited for the bus.

Vince was in his shop. He thought Erika was probably at home. If by some wild flight of imagination you could consider her room a home; from Frances's description it sounded more like a dungeon, and he wondered what kind of crime you had to commit to be sentenced to it. Or on the other hand, she might be spending the day at the art gallery, if you could imagine a square town like Waubonsie having an art gallery.

"You're kidding."

"No, we really have one. Most of the pictures are by local talent and they sort of run to harvest moons and old red barns. There's a woman in the State Bank building who guarantees to teach anyone to paint. But one of the kids who belongs to *Others* has some fairly good stuff on display there—they don't know he's gay of course—and Erika has been trying to find buyers for it." He took both of Frances's hands in his and swung them back and forth, beaming at her with such goodwill that she had to smile back. "Our girl looks like she's coming to life. I won't say she looks happy, that's a lot to expect from a sober chick like Erika, but at least she doesn't seem to be drowning in her own misery. Would this have something to do with you?"

She said, as she had said to Dan Powell, "I'm not sure yet."

"Go easy. That kid's been hurt too much already. But on the other hand, she may never make up her mind if somebody doesn't give her a little push."

"You're a big help."

"I do my best."

"I want to see her—I've got a whole day to myself and I thought maybe she'd like to go somewhere. But her place is way out to hell and gone and I don't know what bus to take. I thought maybe you'd know if she was likely to be home."

"My crystal ball isn't working this morning. I'll take you over, though. I have my roommate's car."

"But the store. Somebody might want to buy something."

"Dreams, just dreams. Anyway, I keep an assistant for these rare moments. Allen!"

A young man looked out of the stockroom. His tousle of hair was bleached a brassy gold and the dark lines at the corners of his eyes were certainly penciled. "Don't tell me you've got a customer," he drawled. "A live one?"

"Certainly not. This is Frances. She belongs to the club."

The boy moved lightly into the shop, hands on hips. "A lovely girl. If I were a female I'd go for her myself."

"If you were any more female I couldn't stand it. I'm going for a ride with this chick. We may never come back. Keep an eye on the stock, will you?"

"You're certainly an optimist. For being willing to drive that heap of David's and for thinking someone might come in." Allen rose *en pointe*, as far as that's possible in Italian sandals. "Have fun, children. I'll stay here and watch the meter tick away the kilowatts. Did you pay the light bill yet?"

"Crazy fool," Vince said, steering Frances out through the back door and into a garbage-cluttered alley where a tired Volkswagen stood. "He's a ballet dancer, home because unemployed. And no, to what you're thinking."

"I wasn't thinking any such thing."

"Oh yes you were. I like my boys butch."

She didn't want to talk about it. "You need somebody to take care of you," she told him, sliding into the little car and marveling as she always did that there was so much more space inside than outside. He looked pleased. "Good, I appeal to your maternal instinct. Would you like to adopt me?"

"Certainly. I'm giving you a bib and a pacifier for Christmas, didn't you know?" She braced herself as the car lurched ahead. "What I'm wondering," she said breathlessly, "why a dancer in Waubonsie? I can take the art gallery—is somebody organizing a corps de ballet too?"

"His family lives here, stupid. He's out of work. They don't like him, but they're too humane to let him starve."

"He should sell plastics." She couldn't keep the bitterness out of her voice. Vince slanted a look at her and decided it was no time to ask questions. He said, "All dancers are crazy. The gay ones are crazier than the rest."

"You don't have to be crazy to be gay, but it helps." She grinned. "It's like being a Negro and converting to Judaism, it's double trouble. Gay and show business too."

"Don't knock it, darling. Use the right bath soap, and romance will enter your life some day."

She locked her hands between her knees to stop them from trembling. "I don't know what I'm going to say to her when I see her."

"Try sign language."

"Oh, shut up."

"Be a good day for a picnic. Get out into the country and smell the new-mown hay." Vince took a deep breath of exhaust fumes and melting asphalt. "To show you what a good-hearted guy I am, I'll lend you David's car if you'll promise to take good care of it."

"David would appreciate that. Why don't you go along? We could stop somewhere and get stuff for sandwiches."

"You feel you need a bodyguard? She might rope you, maybe?"

"Don't be so cute. I'm thinking about the car, I certainly am not going to be responsible for anybody else's car. Besides, she's more likely to say yes if you come too. I don't think she trusts me."

"You shouldn't be so violent," Vince said primly. "I'll come if you really want me, but why are you so anxious about everything? Why don't you wait and see what happens? You might get a happy surprise."

Erika's house looked even tackier in the strong sunlight than it had by moonlight: peeling paint, a strip of roofing torn and flapping, and ragged shades added to the general impression of neglect and decay. Frances said, "The House of Usher," and Vince said, "Charles Addams" in the same breath. "God, we're cultured," Vince said, taking her elbow as they started up the first flight. "Watch out for the banister, it's coming apart. Lean on me and we'll die together."

Erika's door opened before they had time to knock. "The strangest thing," she said smiling. "I thought I heard elephants coming up the stairs. It's the circus?"

"We're looking for the monkey house."

"Come in, anyway."

Vince shook his head. "No, thanks, it's too depressing.

Wouldn't be so bad if you hadn't made your bed, it would at least have that lived-in look."

Frances said, "We came to take you on a picnic."

"That's right. We came to take you out of the straitjacket and smuggle you past the warden."

"I am my own warden," Erika said seriously. "Anyway, I haven't anything to take."

"We're going to buy stuff. Nice cold beer and everything. Come on, don't fight it. David may never trust me with his car again."

Frances thought it was likely, in view of the way he drove. She said earnestly, "Please come. It's a beautiful day."

"All right. You can wait in the hall while I put on some other clothes."

"I like those sexy pants." Vince leered at the wrinkled and faded blue shorts. There was a big three-sided tear over one hip. "Is that the new Italian look?"

"Si, signor."

Frances slipped her arm through Erika's. There was no answering pressure, but at least she didn't pull away. They descended the steps side-by-side, hips moving smoothly in rhythm, feet striking the steps together—scuffed blue sneakers and shabby brown loafers. Vince trailed along behind.

Vince tried again before starting the little car. "Why don't you two chicks go ahead by yourselves? I really have a lot to do at the store."

Erika gave him a look. "Liar. You know nobody ever comes in that store. Except maybe your broke boyfriends."

"Well, it was a good try."

"It's not that we like you," Frances consoled him, "only someone has to carry the food."

He insisted on going into the supermarket alone, leaving the two girls sitting in the car. "He'll buy everything he sees," Erika said dreamily, "Were you the one who thought of this?"

"The picnic was Vince's idea. I just wanted to see you."

"What for?"

Considering the exchanges of pleasure that had left them

both exhausted and relieved two nights before, it seemed a stupid question. Frances looked at her. "Because I like you, silly."

"I wish—" Erika stopped. "you'll be hurt if you get involved with me. That night was wonderful for me, but I'm bad luck. I don't want you to be hurt."

"It would be worth it. Besides, that's not true."

"No. I'm only partly alive."

Frances put a careful arm across her shoulders. "I'll risk it," she said stubbornly. "You're the only one I want."

Vince came out loaded with packages and smiling. "I got a quart of chianti as well as the beer. The beer is in dry ice. And a sausage pizza. The man says it'll stay hot for two hours."

"It won't, I'm starving," Frances said. "What's in all those packages?"

"Pastrami and liverwurst and French bread and bagels and sour tomatoes and some of those big naval oranges from Texas and figs and six cans of beer, big cans. And a few other things."

"Who's going to eat it all?"

"We are."

Erika laughed. Frances left the arm across her shoulder as the car started, and this time she didn't move away. It was enough for now. She would forget everything else and have a good time.

They cut into the stream of traffic leaving town. The state highway was busy but not crowded on this weekday morning. The little car zipped past fields standing tall with corn, pastures where smug cows stood with raised heads meditating, and a bit of fenced-off woodland. Frances looked at comfortable white houses surrounded by their red barns. Would a woman living in a place like that be happy and contented, with a garden and some chickens to keep her busy, or would she hunger for excitement and faraway places?

She supposed it depended on who shared it with you. A life of security and peace might be good for some people, if they shared it with a loved one. It might be fine for Erika, after the terrifying years of her childhood and the nightmare of Kate's violent death. On the other hand, you qualified for that kind of life by having a husband, children, belonging to the Home Bureau. She couldn't see herself or Erika in that setup.

She was still lost in thought when Vince turned off the highway onto a narrow gravel road. "Where are you going?" Erika demanded.

"Damned if I know. Look, there are wild roses. And chicory, that blue stuff. Kind of a corny color combination, isn't it?"

"God has taken no art lessons," Erika reminded him. "There's a whole field of pink stuff. Smells wonderful."

"Clover." The warm breeze was heavy with sweetness. Frances said, "Look, there's a wild canary on the fence."

"Goldfinch."

"They're wild canaries where I come from."

"About the birds I am no expert," Erika said, "but that's definitely a cow looking over the fence at us. I have a feeling she doesn't like us."

"Oh, look, a cemetery!"

"Want to stop and look at it?"

Frances shook her head, but Vince brought the car to a stop anyway. "I'm nuts about these old country graveyards," Vince said. "They make me feel like all life's tied up together somehow. It keeps going on. That's not such a bad feeling."

Erika said, bending her head, "*In mitten des Lebens sind wir im Tode*. I heard that at a funeral."

"Sure, but we're alive now." Vince reached across Frances to give her a pat. "Come on, let's walk around and look at the tombstones. These guys have been dead too long to feel sad for."

It was a very old cemetery, for the middle west.

Eroded slabs of limestone stood at odd angels over graves sunken to ground level; in some cases it was impossible to tell whether they marked the head or foot. Frances said, "And where I come from they call this a burying ground. It's a much nicer way of putting it." She got out of the car and walked through an open place in the low iron fence. Two narrow tracks still marked the place where cars or perhaps buggies had gone in and out, long ago. "I wonder who took the gate away? Look, some of the graves have been mowed."

"Probably the grandchildren or great-grandchildren of the original settlers still live close by. You know, the Scotch and English came here first—then the Norwegians and Germans, starting around 1850. Some of the Germans fled with Carl Schurz after the revolution of 1848. I read a book about it," Vince said, sounding apologetic.

Frances bent to read the carving on a stone. "Senath Adams, wife of Jacob, born January 10, 1810, died June 22, 1891. She had a good long life, anyhow."

Erika said softly, "It is so peaceful here."

It was peaceful, Frances thought, stepping further into the grassy acre. Fine dust rose under her shoes; she could see the sole prints on the narrow path. Long feathery grass stirred in the hot summer air. A patch of wild roses edged one of the plots; their flat petals were spread wide to the sun, the centers pure gold. Birds chirped from a row of trees at the back of the cemetery, and a tractor hummed in the distance. The sound seemed right. Frances knew without seeing him what the driver looked like, shirtsleeves rolled up over bunchy arm muscles, one of those little striped caps pulled down over his eyes, riding high and easy over land his grandfather had stepped off behind a plow.

Vince went from plot to plot, trying not to step on the graves. "It doesn't seem respectful. I know they don't care, it's the idea behind it. Go ahead, laugh."

But no one laughed. Erika looked at him tenderly.

"Look, here's one of my ancestors."

"How come?"

"He has my name, anyway." Frances dropped to her knees for a better look. "It's poetry, too." The letters were worn almost even with the pitted stone. "'John Orrin Kirby, born in Somerset, England, 1834. Died in Will County, Illinois, of the fever in the twentieth year of his life. O cruel Death that would no longer spare a loving one to mother, father, brothers, sisters dear. He was a stranger and we took him in.'"

"Poor boy."

"He could have been my—what? Great-grandfather?"

Vince said, "He was only twenty, he probably wasn't anybody's great-grandfather."

"Relative, anyway. I sort of see what you mean. It's like Zen."

"Sure, all life is one."

Erika had said nothing. She bent and began to pick the wild roses, handling them carefully because the tough little stems were thickly set with thorns. When she had seven or eight she tied them together with a long piece of grass, pulling the ends into a stiff bow. She laid the nosegay on the boy's grave.

Vince asked, "What's all this?"

"He was so far away from home."

"They were all far away from home. They all came over to make a new life. We do the same thing—it only looks different."

"They were lucky," Erika said. "My people are in limepits and trenches and—I don't know, maybe someone alive, I don't know if they are dead or alive. My mother and father and my little brother, Kurt. The Red Cross tried, everybody tried." She gave him a cold look. "This boy was like me, he was alone. The others had families."

"None of us have anybody," Vince said seriously, "until we find someone to love. That's what everybody is looking for, someone to belong to."

Frances felt uneasy. She said, "I'm hungry. The beer's going to get warm and the pizza's going to get cold if we don't eat pretty soon."

"All right." Erika dusted her hands on the already dingy seat of her shorts. "Let's go outside the fence, though. It makes my appetite go away to be in such a sad place."

"In China they used to put food on the graves instead of flowers," Vince reminded her.

"That was for the spirits, though."

"Yes, but beggars ate it."

Vince waited until the girls were outside the fence, then followed them. "David even has a blanket in this car. I don't know what he uses it for. I hope I remembered to get a can opener, too."

Frances laughed. It was a relief to be back in the sunshine, out of the cemetery shade. "You'll make a fine wife for some nice boy," she told him, taking the can of beer he handed her. "What's holding up the pizza?"

13 "I'VE PUT ON TEN POUNDS SINCE THIS MORN-ing," Frances looked with desire at the last slice of pizza, covered with golden cheese and dark crumbles of sausage, and decided she couldn't eat it. "Not another bite. Now I know why farmers' wives get fat. It's the fresh country air."

"It's the fresh country eggs and cream and stuff," Vince said. "Farmers don't eat pizza."

"I don't think any of us know anything about it," Frances said. She drained the last few drops from her beer can and added it to the little pile of debris which Erika said they must bury before they left. "I'd like to take a nap. I can't even move."

"Go right ahead, honey. Nobody's going to bother you, they only use this road on Decoration Day. I'm going for a walk. A nice long walk," Vince said meaningfully, looking at Erika. "I won't be back for a couple of hours."

Erika scowled at him. He smiled innocently. "I love to commune with nature," he assured her, and sauntered off, swinging his arms and looking chipper in spite of grass stains and dust.

Frances stretched out on the blanket, pillowing her head on her arm so she could look at Erika. "It's funny how the fresh air relaxes you," she said idly. "They ought to bottle it for tension cases. It's better than tranquilizers."

Erika's face was grave. "I don't like it. It frightens me. Whenever you start feeling safe, something always happens. Suddenly and when you're not looking."

"If it's going to happen, it'll happen anyway. I know what you mean," Frances admitted, remembering premonitions of her own, "but expecting the worst is no help. The things you think about hardly ever happen anyhow. It's always something you never gave any thought to."

"I don't mean separate happenings." Erika couldn't explain what she did mean, or perhaps she felt it would be useless to argue. She sat on the very edge of the blanket, as far from Frances as she could get, arms wrapped around her bare knees. "Take a nap if you want to. I won't talk."

"How about you, aren't you sleepy?"

"Maybe a little."

"Then lie down and take a nap, stupid."

"A car might come along."

"Well, they're not going to run over us. We're way off the road. And we haven't got anything worth stealing, nobody would even look twice at the car. Are you afraid some farmer's going to pick it up and carry it home on his tractor?"

"One almost could." Erika smiled. "I like these little ones, they're so nice and plan. Not big ones with fancy trimmings, ugh."

"They're not so expensive, either." Frances wondered how it would feel to have a car of her own, come and go as she pleased. Until now it hadn't mattered—there was no place she wanted to go. Now she thought, if I had a secretarial job I could make payments on one of these and go places, vacations and all. She felt that she wouldn't mind counting pennies, eating left-overs and budgeting for the rent. Never had enough money to get used to spending it. She had been too concerned with other things to care about the stuff women buy to make themselves believe they are safe and happy. A woman goes shopping to fill empty time—no other reason. If she were with someone she cared about, she wouldn't mind making every pound of ham-burger do the work of three pounds of steak. Frances sighed.

Erika asked, "What are you thinking about?"

"Nothing really. Why don't you take a nap? Nothing terrible is going to happen if you shut your eyes for half an hour."

"But that's exactly the way I feel," Erika said, sounding sur-prised. "How did you know? At night I can't sleep, and in the daytime I feel, well, I don't know how to tell you, I'm walk-ing in my sleep. I have to get over it before school starts." She turned away so that her back was to Frances. "I went to a doctor and she gave me some pills, but they made me feel terrible."

"Sleep last night?"

"Yes." There was resentment in Erika's voice. "Why are you doing this to me?"

"It doesn't have anything to do with me. You get over things by yourself, after a while." That sounded smug, and she wasn't sure it was true. "Look, you have another fifty years to live. You might as well make something of it."

"O cruel death that would no longer spare," Erika said softly. "The dead are lucky, their troubles are over."

"Is that why you put the flowers on the boy's grave? I thought you were feeling sorry for him."

It was a low blow. Dislike showed in Erika's face. "I was, I was sorry for him because of the way he died," she said in such a small voice Frances could hardly make out the words. "Maybe I'll go to sleep too."

"Sure, why don't you?" Frances lay unmoving, careful not to startle her, while she stretched out on the far edge of the blanket. Without turning her head she knew exactly how Erika looked, how her face looked with the eyes shut and the small freckles spattered across her cheeks. She knew what Erika would look like stripped of the blue shorts and cotton shirt, her body flat and white against the blanket.

"Frances?"

"Yes."

"What do you want from me?"

"I don't think I want anything, yet, except to love you."

"I don't want anyone to love me."

"I'm sorry, I can't help it. People don't do these things on purpose."

She had to admit that Erika might be right. Life would certainly be easier, if not happier, without emotions. That was why so many people tried to stay up on the surface, finding their greatest anxiety in overdue bills and their greatest pleasure in buying things. The trouble was, once you had a taste of something better you knew the difference. No one got along without feelings. If you eliminated love, the space would be taken up by resentment or despair or something much worse.

I've been living a totally false life, she thought. It can't go on. I'll tell him tomorrow.

Erika said suddenly, "You know about Kate, don't you? Maybe I asked you that before."

"Vince told me."

"We were going to be together as long as we lived. Through all our middle age, and everything."

"I'm sorry. But you made her happy."

"I can't start all over again, and lose everything. It's too difficult. I can't take the risk."

Life is insecure for everyone, Frances thought, but she kept her tone light. "Going to live in a vacuum for the next fifty years?"

"It scares me to think about you."

"Then don't." Patches of sunshine filtered through the branches and lay in leaf-shaped patters of warmth on her arms and legs. The heat felt good. High above, the leaves made a soft summery rustling. Frances closed her eyes.

"I can't help it. I think about you all the time. Why did you stay that night? Why did you do what you did? I don't like to feel so close to anyone."

"I'm not pushing you. I won't do anything you don't want me to."

Erika sat up. Frances glinted a look at her; she looked very stiff and straight. "That's the trouble, I wanted you to. I want you right now, at this moment. I am ashamed."

"Well," Frances said slowly, "if I thought you were really ashamed I'd go away. It wouldn't do you any good though. Sooner or later you're going to need someone. It might as well be me."

Erika sighed. "I should have been the one who died." Her face was set in misery. "Kate was unhappy all her life until I found her," she said slowly. "You don't know what it was like for her. She had such a short time for being happy."

"Do you think she'd have been happy with you gone? Do you think she'd have wanted you to feel like this?"

"I can't help it."

Frances rolled over on her back and lay with her eyes open, watching the leaves that now moved almost imperceptibly; the light shimmered and changed. She felt at once wide awake and calm. The coarse weave of the green blanket, the rippled texture on the bark of the tree beyond Erika, the pebbly gravel of the country road all stood out in sharp relief. Erika lay with her knees pulled up, her arms thrown out at different angles, her bosom hardly lifting the soft cotton shirt. There was a touching immaturity about the slight curves of her breasts and the small tight buds; she no longer seemed like a boy, but like a very young girl just beginning to develop out of childhood. Frances wanted to put protective hands over her bosom. She said, without moving, "Shut your eyes and try to sleep."

"I wish I could stay here all night."

"I do too. That room of yours is nobody's dream castle."

"You know what I wish?" Erika asked dreamily. "I'm ashamed. I wish you could go back with me and stay by my bed till I go to sleep. That's silly. Oh God, I don't know what I wish." She sat up and pushed back her short hair in distraction, scowling at Frances, "I'm all mixed up."

Blow hot and blow cold, Frances thought; but she'd done too much of that herself to blame anyone else. She said, "I'll go back with you if you want me to, and I'll do anything you want me to and nothing you don't. Because I love you. Now shut up and lie down."

"You're good to me."

"Sure, I'm great." And how is she going to feel when she finds out about Bill? Frances wondered.

She reached out a hand. Erika put her thin fingers into it, like a child. They were cold in spite of the day, but they warmed gradually, and Frances could feel the little pulse in the wrist beating in unison with her own. It was the first time Erika had made a move toward her of her own accord. In bed she had been frightened, then resigned, then responsive and passionate—but this reaching out meant more than all that had happened during that evening.

Erika said in a whisper, "I want to be close to you."

Frances moved over and gathered her in. Holding Erika tightly, she could feel the slight trembling of that small body, as if Erika were lying in a cool wind. Now there was no hesitation. She smoothed the delicate shoulders with her hand, murmuring words that made no sense. Erika lay passive. But when the caresses deepened in intensity and the hand reached farther, she lay back on the wool blanket, ready and welcoming Frances's aggressiveness. The leaf shadows sifted down, dark and light in a fantastic pattern against the white skin, the reddish-blonde hair, and on Frances's darker hands moving rhythmically. Her face was serious with only one intention: to bring fulfillment to the one she loved.

In the distance the humming of the tractor was like a gigantic insect song.

"You make me feel so safe," Erika said when the spasm of feeling was over and she lay relaxed again in the circle of Frances's arms. She closed her eyes, then opened them again. "Here—button me up," she suggested smiling.

In no time at all she was asleep.

Frances lay unmoving, holding her as though she might break. An ant climbed over the edge of the blanket and began making its way, slowly and with determination, over the cloth of Erika's sneaker. Frances lay watching, hypnotized by its precision and tiny energy, until her own eyes began to close heavily.

14

"I DON'T KNOW WHY I EVER MOVED INTO THIS terrible place," Erika said. She stood beside the little car with her hand on the door, looking with distaste at the crumbling old house. "It's depressing."

Vince said, "You wanted to be depressed, remember?" With the grass stains on the seat of his pants, dust-coated moccasins and purple spots on his shirt (you have to be Greek to drink from a bottle without dribbling, he said, or Spanish), he remained an elegant and fastidious-looking young man, Frances smiled at him. Let him say it, let him antagonize Erika by scolding her. She couldn't. She had too much to lose. She would have to be patient and understanding, even though patience was never natural to her.

The house was certainly depressing. So was the landlady, whom they met on the way up—a small woman with a tight girdle, a small bitter face and purple black hair with a metallic glint like a beetle's back. A hard little woman who gave them a suspicious insect-like look from pouchy eyes and shut her lips tightly in answer to Vince's "Howdy." Frances had never seen the other tenants, but she could imagine. She said, "What worries me about this place, it's a firetrap. One fool smoking in bed could burn it down in ten minutes."

Erika shrugged. "What has to happen will happen."

"You could be somewhere else when it happens."

"Don't nag."

The halls were dimly lighted, fifteen-watt bulbs with a crusting of flyspecks. The wainscot and door frames were of gloomy dark wood. Frances ran a hand over the stair railing and brought it away smudged with greasy dust.

In Erika's room the bulbs were bright and the woodwork had been dusted, but everything was old.

The bed sagged, the scrim curtains had been washed several times too often and hung limp at dusty windows. Erika said defensively, "Anyway, the bed's clean. I take the sheets to the laundromat myself. And there is a plastic cover on the mattress." As though heartbreak could be endured, but not dirt.

"Are you hungry? I have soup. Or I can go to the store."

Frances sighed. "I don't want to eat for at least a week. All that pizza. All those sour pickles."

"The store closes at nine," Vince reminded them.

"It can't be that late!"

Erika glanced at the alarm clock on the dresser. "Twenty minutes after nine. It stays light a long time now."

A good thing too, for lonely women who had trouble sleeping. Frances knew what it was like to dread the long winter evenings when darkness settled down before five, and ten o'clock felt like late night. She said, "It was a good day, wasn't it?"

"While it lasted," Vince said. "I have to go, dolls. David might not miss me, but he will worry about the car."

They stood apart, listening to him clattering down the stairs. Frances said, dreamily, "Vince is sweet."

"My best friend."

They looked at each other. It was a self-conscious moment: there were too many things to say, and no way to say any of them without inflicting hurt. Frances felt embarrassed, as though she were being thrown into intimacy with a stranger. Her arms prickled with sunburn, her face felt dusty, she was conscious of vague aches here and there. She said stiffly, "If you've changed your mind and don't want me to stay, I won't."

"This is such an ugly place. I wish we could sleep outdoors. It would be nice when the stars came out."

"We'll go on a camping trip some time."

"Don't talk to me about some time."

She let that lie. The obvious next step was to say, "Then you come home with me." Erika was expecting it, waiting with a look of bright expectancy. Frances considered what would happen if she took Erika into that house—with Bill's clothes and shaving things all over the place, the connubial double bed, haunted by Bill's lovemaking; the dread that Bill would be home any minute. Furtive, sneaky. It was impossible at this delicate point to explain that yes, she had a husband (twenty-one years, for God's sake), and no, she certainly didn't love him, never had; and yes, she planned to leave him as soon as she could gather up enough courage. And yes, she did love Erika with all her heart, but in the meantime she had been going to bed regularly with this man.

It was impossible. She hoped, not too brightly, that Erika was taking for granted a flat shared with a friend (purely platonic) or an aging mother. She considered saying, "We could go to my place, but it would disturb my mother." No good, she was a poor liar.

She said, "Do you want to go to a hotel? I have enough money."

"I hate hotels."

They looked at each other. Erika said, "Nobody could really love me, not anymore. It was different with her. She needed me—and besides I was a different person then."

"I need you too."

"You want me. It's not the same."

Frances said rather crossly, "There's no law against wanting, is there? Or both at once. It's so silly to fight like this. If you want me to go away, say so and I'll go."

"I'm going to make some coffee."

Let her; it would give her something to do. Frances sat down on the side of the bed and slipped off her loafers. She sat smiling a little, looking around the room.

The closet door stood open on a collection of dark skirts and tailored blouses, a heavy coat, and one rather shabby tweed suit that looked limp on its hanger. Shorts and slacks hung on hooks. Beneath, a pair of snow boots, a second pair of sneakers—like the ones she was wearing, but white—some loafers and a pair of black pumps with low heels, rather run down. That was all. Not exactly what the well-dressed white collar girl wore, if you could believe the movies.

In addition to the alarm clock the dresser top displayed a comb and plastic hairbrush, lipstick, jar of cold cream; also a small spiral notebook and a green fountain pen. Frances guessed that if she were to open the drawers of the dresser—one of those bosomy old numbers with a swinging mirror—most of them would be empty. She also guess that everything Erika owned would be plain, and old to the point of falling apart, and this would be due not to her poverty—teachers in the public schools don't earn much, but they do buy clothes—but because she didn't care. Or she was trying to punish herself for something. For being alive, when Kate was dead?

Erika came back with the pot of water and put it to heat on the little electric plate, moving absently, going through the familiar motions with her mind somewhere else. "It takes a long time to heat," she said, a hostess making conversation. Frances said, "It always does." This coffee bit was bringing back her first visit to Erika's room, the evening that started with such high hopes and ended in an early departure and no progress at all. She wished she hadn't thought of it.

Erika said suddenly, "I'm afraid."

"That makes two of us."

"What have you got to be afraid of?"

"Losing you."

"That's no loss. I really am not worth having."

"You don't know a thing about it."

Erika looked at her somberly. "I wasn't going to see you again. I seem to have no willpower."

"That's good." Frances got up from the sagging bed and walked barefoot across the floor. The rug was gritty under her feet. Erika turned away from her, reaching for the two plastic cups. Frances stood looking, not at her but at the coffee fussing and spitting inside the little glass dome. "It needs another minute or so."

"That's right."

Frances gave her a sharp look. The calm and rested look of the afternoon was gone. Erika's mouth was narrow with apprehension; the skin seemed stretched thin over her cheekbones. Frances said, "Don't look like that. I'm not going to do anything you don't want me to."

"That's what I hate about it," Erika said sullenly. "I want you to stay. I want you to make love to me, damn it. I want you to be a little bit violent." She looked at the floor. "It's all wrong. My body has no right to do this to me."

"Not wrong at all, no more than eating when you're hungry."

"I don't mean that way. I never could see why any kind of loving was bad, not as long as the people like each other. But now I don't want to want anybody." She shivered. "It's a mess."

Frances took the cups out of her hand and set them down on the table. She put her arms around Erika and held her close, feeling her begin to tremble. She said, "Believe me, all I want is for you to be happy. Do you have to think ahead all the time? Can't you be happy right now?"

When the mind holds back, the only way is to persuade the body.

She smoothed back the fair hair that curled in damp weather and when Erika perspired. It was in tendrils now. With one arm she held Erika close against her while she unbuttoned the cotton shirt and ran and inquiring hand over the smooth skin of her sides and breasts. Erika's breathing deepened. Her small hard nipples stood up rigidly, and the beating of her heart accentuated in the fine, thin cage of her ribs. She said in a thready whisper, "Oh God, darling."

One thing about summer, Frances thought light headedly, there's not so much to take off. She managed it with one hand, still keeping Erika in the circle of her other arm, pressed close against her. The torn blue shorts fell to the floor. She sent her own skirt and two bits of white cotton to join them.

"You don't want the light off, do you?"

"No, I like to look at you."

Under the pink cotton spread, the sheets were smooth and warm. She turned the top one back, the spread with it. She pulled Erika to her so that their bodies fitted together like parts of one person. They moved together, with no thought left and no feeling except the need and the excitement that rose higher and higher in both of them, like a flood, until it drowned out everything else.

When her hand reached the most secret place, she found Erika open and warm and ready for her. "Make me," Erika said. Her eyes were shut tight but her face was intense with desire. "Make me do it. Don't stop."

15 IT WAS DAY. FRANCES RAISED UP ON ONE elbow to take a closer look, not sure that the light pressing against the window wasn't moonlight or the glow from a street lamp, hoping against hope that she had only dozed off for an hour or two. She had to go home. She

wondered whether Bill would be half drunk and triumphant, with a contract in his pocket, or disappointed and quite drunk. She wondered whether it was, maybe, two in the morning with a full moon.

But she knew.

It was after six. She knew even before she rolled to the edge of the bed and looked at the clock. There was a morning freshness in the air, and some small bird had begun a well-meant chirping in the tree outside the window; it was his reiterated complaint that had broken into her dreams. Delivery trucks were rolling down the street on their way to replenish grocery stores and butcher shops. It was full morning.

Early light lay over the room like cold water, neither hiding nor softening the beat-up old furniture but only adding a layer to it, like a coat of transparent varnish. She puzzled a moment over something on the floor beside the bed: a heap of clothes, left there when she began to catch and hold Erika's moment of unwilling passion. At the memory, she closed her eyes and took a deep breath. I didn't think she was going to make it, Frances thought with a small smile, but we got her over the hump that time.

No man would have had the patience; many girls wouldn't. She didn't know, yet, what it would be like next time, whether Erika's reluctance on the brink of completion was a part of her pattern or whether it was the last stand of her death wish. She might wake up feeling wonderful, melting with happiness. She might wake hating herself and everyone else, ready to burrow deeper into loneliness because she'd had a breath of joy and it was more than she could bear. Some people were like that. It was a chance you had to take.

Erika slept. She had hardly moved since Frances snapped off the light and pulled up the sheet, as they lay sweaty and short of breath after the final and most terrible effort. Erika's body barely lifted the thin material. She breathed slowly, lying on her side with her knees pulled up as though washed ashore by a strong tide. Her face was calm and open. Frances felt a wave of tenderness for her, as though Erika were a child who had been sick to the point of death and was past her crisis.

She wanted to stay here, to turn over and lie close to Erika, to take the girl in her arms and feel the soft sweetness of her and marvel over the way her body was put together. It was impossible. She had to get out of here and go back to a house where she didn't belong, where an angry and baffled man would be waiting for her. At the thought of the trouble she was about to stir up, her skin crawled. But there was no help for it. She had reached the point of no return.

For all the pleasure she felt with her accomplishments in bed, she was tired. Her eyes ached, her neck was stiff and her teeth felt fuzzy. One good argument in favor of living together, she decided, was to have a toothbrush handy when you needed it. She needed a bath, too. The idea of the tub across the hall, grimed by God-knows-who, revolted her. Even if you scrubbed it shiny, the ghosts of a hundred other tenants would still be there. This for the gentle Erika was not to be borne. I'll get her out of here, she resolved.

She was sitting on the edge of the bed, trying to gather enough willpower to get dressed, when she realized that Erika was awake. She turned around. "Hi. Did I wake you?"

"Where are you going?"

"I have to go now. I'll come back as soon as I can. Maybe before noon."

Erika shut her eyes again. "I'll be here all day," she said in a small pleased voice. "I don't want to see anybody but you."

Frances leaned over and kissed her neck. Erika opened her eyes. "You don't have to ask me today, do you?"

"I hope not."

"Go now, so you can come back."

There was nobody in the hall or on the steps; the building was still asleep. When she stepped on the porch she could tell that it was going to be another sultry day. The sun was well up and there were men on the sidewalk with lunch buckets, going to work; even a few women in jeans and bandannas.

In the next big block, she could see the Rexall sign and the big red A&P sign glistening in the early sunshine. A man was carrying a tier of big flat pans into the grocery; the top one was filled with sweet rolls in cellophane. The sight made her hungry. She thought it over, looking at the electric-eye door after he had gone in. Bill would be at the Regent Street house, sullenly awake or soddenly asleep depending on how much he'd had to drink. In either case she was in trouble. She felt she could face him, since it was the last time; but not without a cup of good, hot coffee.

The drugstore was closed, but the all-night diner a couple of doors away stood open to the early sun and wind, mixing a smell of frying grease with the dawn breeze. She went in. Two Mexicans were having breakfast at once end of the counter, speaking softly in Spanish. She sat down at the other end, seeing the counterman look at her wrinkled clothes and uncombed hair but not caring much what he thought. "Just coffee, black."

He would figure that she'd been out all night and was hung over—but it was her own business, and hers and that of whatever man had kept her up until this hour. Hell, he might even be sympathetic if he knew the real story. She looked closely to see if he might be one of the boys and decided that he wasn't.

For the ten-thousandth time she wondered why people pry into other people's private affairs. Maybe because they're not satisfied with what they have? The happy ones don't care what you do, they may make a joke about it but they're not mean, they wish you well. It was the cold bitter ones, the women—oh, the women could be evil, the ones who had never been stirred to any real emotion, they had to make trouble for anyone who seemed happy. Those, and the ones who want a girl but are afraid to admit it even to themselves, and then men who beat up gay boys because they have to be reassured of their own maleness. They're the ones who make trouble. The cold ones and the scared ones.

The coffee was hot and good. The counterman brought her a tiny bottle of cream, the way they always did, and she pushed it aside and concentrated on the hot, bitter goodness. Wondering why coffee was always good where a lot of men ate and terrible at women's affairs; the more genteel the function, the weaker the coffee. It was one way to keep her mind off the moment when she would have to face Bill.

She got up stiffly, leaving change on the counter, and walked back into the bright sunlight. Dreading the thought of returning home and facing Bill, she waited nervously on the corner for the Main Street bus. When it came she got on it and sat down behind two young girls in workingslacks, their hair pincurled under flowered babushkas. The spent the ride making up their faces. Femininity victorious on the assembly line.

She was afraid. Might as well admit it. She had never been this afraid in the days with Bake, not even when she thought she was planning to leave Bill and move into Bake's apartment, because Bake was strong. Bake would take care of her. But Erika, although she had a resilient toughness of her own (or how would she have lasted this long?), needed to be looked after just now. It was up to her, Frances. She had to be brave enough for two, and God knew she wasn't built for it.

She transferred on Main Street where the counterman had said, and sat glumly looking out of the windows at the still-closed stores and the big gloomy churches and bright little eating places hot with electric lights. Rooming houses and small factories skirted the business district; then modest family houses and then, coming into the open, the comfortable green-ness and gentility of the neighborhoods where the well-to-do lived. Bill was right. Most women would think they were lucky to live out here in the snug, smug suburbs.

I'm not one of them, she thought with a qualm of pure fright. Never was, never will be. It's no use knocking myself out trying.

Her block was stirring awake. Women would be fixing breakfast in their bright modern kitchens; the live-in maid was a thing of the past for all but a few; machines did the work. At the worst I could be somebody's cleaning woman, she thought, half meaning it; I'm neat and handy around a house. I wouldn't starve.

She put her shoulders back and marched briskly up to the front porch, with a briskness calculated to show anybody who might be looking that she was not only sober but happy and full of self-confidence.

Bill was up. An almost empty fifth of bourbon was on the small table beside him, and his face had the mauve puffy look it got when he had too much to drink. He looked up when she came in, looked away, and then stood up to face her. He said, slowly and a little thickly, "It's about time, you tramp."

She wanted to lie. She had always lied to him before, all of her good resolutions swept away by fright. Pa had looked like this when he came home on payday, drunk on the grocery money. A fear learned early lasts long. It was skinny little Frankie Kirby who stood holding onto the doorframe of the Regent Street house, as she had clung to the door in the dingy little company house.

But only for a moment. She thought of Erika, smiling and half-asleep, waiting for her to come back, and her hands tightened into fists in the folds of her skirt. Do this for Erika. If she failed now they would both go down.

"What's your story this time? Don't believe a word you tell me, not a word, all those other times you handed me a lot of bullshit." He scowled at her. "This better be good."

She cleared her throat. "Bill, I haven't been honest with you and I'm sorry. I mean, I tried. All this last year since Bob was married. I don't love you and you don't really give a damn about me, it's just the idea." She gulped. "I'm leaving. Now, today."

"You're crazy."

She saw, with wonder, that he was about to cry, whether with anger or shock or drunken sentiment she didn't know. It was even possible that he loved her, so far as he could love anyone.

He spoke again. "We've been getting along fine. You had a spell back there, but that was over a long time ago. We get along better than most people."

It was the same old stone wall. She could explain until she was dizzy, but she couldn't get through to him. He'd built up this image of the happy marriage, right out of the women's mags. All she could do in self-defense was break it into little pieces.

She heard her voice harsh in the quiet house. "I've been faking, Bill. I'll never be able to live with a man, any man. It isn't your fault, you've been all right, but I can't make it. I'm a lesbian."

"Oh hell, Francie, I may not be the most romantic guy in the world, but we get along all right. This is some notion you've picked up out of a book or something. Tell you what it is, women get this way when they start to get middle aged." He looked relieved.

"I've hated it all along. I'm a lesbian, Bill. You might as well believe it, because it's true."

Her eyes were wet. He said reluctantly, "All right, supposing that's true. You could go to a psychiatrist. That's their job, to make people normal."

"I don't need a psychiatrist. This isn't a mental illness, it's just the way I am."

"You've found someone to have an affair with."

"Maybe."

He dropped the glass. The liquor spread over the new rug. He paid no attention. He took a couple of steps toward her, walking carefully. "You have, haven't you? Don't lie to me."

"I'm sorry."

His face hardened. She moved back a step. Not a man to hit anybody, she had told herself yesterday (a million years ago), but there had been that horrible afternoon she tried not to remember, when her coldness infuriated him and he stripped her and took her with a violence that was like rape. To be violated now would be more than she could bear, with the touch of Erika still on her skin, the taste of Erika on her lips. She glanced behind her, through the open hall door. Innocent sunshine lay across the porch. If she turned and ran screaming down the steps, neighbors would surely come—she would be safe.

She stood where she was.

He hit her. Rocked off balance, she went numb for a second. Then she was standing against the wall with a hand to her jaw, while pain spread up into her face and down into her chest. Before she could breathe the second blow caught her across the cheek. The edge of his palm caught her eyes, and lights flashed.

She said, "You bastard." Her voice came out blurred. Salt trickled into her mouth. She spat it out, a red blob.

"I won't let you get a divorce."

"You might as well. I'm going anyway."

"I'll tell the truth in court."

"Go ahead."

He looked doubtful. She knew that by this time tonight his determination would have melted; he would be thinking about his job, his reputation, the publicity in the papers. Poor guy, she thought, he works so hard for security, and there isn't any.

Pain throbbed in from her chin. She felt the place carefully. It was swelling, all right. It would almost surely be discolored, but she didn't think anything was broken. Maybe it was a small price to pay for freedom. Maybe it was a pattern she had to repeat every time she changed her life. Her father had blacked an eye for her, learning that she was going to college on a scholarship; she had arrived on campus with a spectacular shiner. And all the pancake makeup in the world wouldn't cover the bruises she carried to Bob's wedding, the day after that session with the lady baseball player.

She said, "Let me by. I want to pack my clothes."

He looked at her. At what she saw in his eyes, she was afraid. Then he picked up a book from the table and threw it as hard as he could, not at her but at the wall. It hit with a smack and fell, fluttering loose pages. Bill pushed past her and went out, slamming the door. His five-minute stand as a man was over.

She stood still, held by the sound of the banged door. In a minute she heard the car start. It rolled down the drive in reverse, stopped, righted itself and off. Frances laughed. The sound was loud in the house.

He would go somewhere and have a few more drinks, maybe find some nice sympathetic bartender to tell his troubles to. And when he sobered up, he would probably decide to forgive her all over again. That was the American male in real life, no guts. He'd be back, reasonable and kind, and when that failed, pitiful. She could be worn down by pathos, when all the mink stole and charge account arguments failed; especially if she was tired to begin with.

She locked the front door and bolted it, went through the house to the kitchen and put on the night lock. Climbing up the back stair she remembered, wondering, that she had always been afraid of physical violence. Now she felt clear headed and triumphant, as though she had come through a crisis and the rest would be easy.

She put some alcohol on her bruised chin while the bath-tub filled. The jaw was certainly swollen, and a plum-colored lump was beginning to darken just under her chin. The right eye looked ominous too. She blinked a couple of times; her vision was all right, so it was probably only the lid. Her teeth were intact and nothing seemed to be broken. I got out of that pretty well, she thought smugly, peeling off her clothes and stepping into the tub. And since cruelty was the commonest ground for divorce in Illinois, it wouldn't be necessary to fake any evidence. She would get to a lawyer while she still had the bruises to prove it.

Bathed, shampooed, dried and dressed in clean slacks and a thin shirt, she began sorting her clothes. Hurry, but don't panic; they were good clothes and it might be a long time before she could afford to buy more. No Mrs. William Ollenfield stuff, no little flowered dresses with ruffles, just the things that felt good on her, office casuals, shoes she could walk in, no jewelry except her diamond—she supposed she had a right to that, she would sell it later. The winter clothes could be packed and sent to her after things settled down. She supposed she had done enough housework to earn them even if she hadn't been too satisfactory in bed. She felt calm and executive as she folded her things and laid them in the suitcases.

She tucked her hoard of small bills into the front of her bra and slipped a checkbook into the back pocket of her slacks. The bank wasn't open until half-past nine, and even if it occurred to Bill to close out the joint checking account she would be there, first in line when the doors opened. She would make a scene; he wouldn't. She didn't think he would give the money a thought;

anyway, he was probably feeling penitent by this time. In a way it was too bad she didn't want a property settlement. That sock in the jaw would have gone a long way in court.

She looked around the bedroom. It didn't mean anything, it was just a room; faced with a choice between it and Erika's hideous little cell she could leave those fancy drapes without a qualm. She picked up Bob's graduation picture and opened her large suitcase to put it in. Sentimental, but she hoped he would go on liking her if he didn't approve of her. It was her turn to take the long step into an independent adult life, and it was badly overdue. Bob was a person in his own right now, his life interwoven with that of Mari and the coming child. If they met again it must be as friends or strangers. Still, she would take his picture with her.

The telephone was ringing in the downstairs hall. She walked past it, carrying her two heavy suitcases. At the front door she put them down and dug the house keys out of her pocket. She laid them down on the small table beside the lamp, half a dozen keys on a metal ring with a scroll *F* in black enamel on the tag; she turned it face up and turned the lamp on so that Bill wouldn't miss them.

She set her suitcases on the porch, checked the lock, then stepped out and pulled the door shut behind her. The Yale lock clicked shut with a small definite sound. Inside, the telephone was still ringing.

She walked down the narrow strip of concrete that bisected the yard, a bag in each hand. At the edge of the sidewalk she hesitated. Then she went on to the corner, without looking back.

16 HEAT ROSE FROM THE DOWNTOWN STREETS and shimmered in the sunlight. People moved slowly; women in the shops seemed to be filling up their time rather than buying, they carried few packages and they looked listlessly at merchandise held out by mechanical clerks, as though they really didn't care. Drugstore fountains were full of people resting their feet, having cold drinks and

enjoying the air-conditioning. Cooled stores did a good business in notions, cosmetics, small items that gave people an excuse for loitering. It was an average midwestern summer.

Frances brushed through the drifting people as though she belonged to another race. Her mind was on neither weather nor shopping.

Today her decisions were taking shape without conscious effort, rising into her mind as though someone else were telling her what to do. She checked her suitcase into a locker at the Greyhound station, unremarked among the people coming and going. With the key in one pants' pocket and her checkbook in the other, she moved on to the bank, made out a check payable to cash for a hundred dollars, then tore it up and made out another for two hundred. She had to think about Erika, too. She told herself calmly, standing in line at the teller's window, that she would be working by the time it was gone. When she got out on the street she tore the rest of the checks across the middle and threw them into a city wastebasket.

It had taken a long time to gather up enough courage for the first step. That taken, she was going right ahead. She marveled at how easy it was.

It was almost eleven by the big clock on the bank building. She felt pleasantly hungry. She stuffed her tens and twenties into the breast pocket of her shirt and buttoned the flap down over the bulge; that made her look lopsided. From the change in her purse she bought a newspaper and went into the drugstore. The fountain was busy, but she climbed onto the last empty stool and folded her paper back to the For Rent columns. Over bacon and eggs and a toasted pecan roll she checked everything that looked halfway possible. Settled, she could look for a job. There were always jobs, in good times and bad, and she was young enough and attractive enough to fall into one. If she didn't like it she could change later.

She supposed she would have to get word to Bill before she did another thing. Left to himself he'd have the entire police force out looking for her. She didn't want to spoil her chances of a quick, easy divorce by being counter-sued for desertion;

but she felt Bill needed a few hours in which to simmer down. She would ask Vince to call him. Vince would know which lawyer to see, too. She counted on him to help her, if not for her own sake, then for Erika's.

The town, which had seemed so cramped and alien a few weeks ago, now began to take on a welcoming look. Since Erika had a contract for the coming school year they would have to stay here for a while, at least. She would work in one of these downtown office buildings, and the people she met would be friends, at least during working hours. Any dealings she might have from straight people would always have to be limited by the necessity for caution, but even so, the idea of working with other people was pleasant after so many years alone. She would find a place to live, a place to get her hair done, a store for buying her office dresses, a corner where she could wait for the bus that took her to work. She would get a card at the library and come to know the librarians and where her favorite books were on the shelves.

She felt wonderful.

She thought about Erika and found with surprise that there was no hurry about seeing her. They had years and years ahead of them.

She got a handful of dimes from the cashier and began calling the people who had apartments to rent, skipping those who didn't mention the rental or the number of rooms. Two were already taken, a third was looking for a man (men were more reliable about paying, a female whine at the other end said; she hung up before she could lose her temper). Another was at the far end of town, fine for people with cars but no good for anyone who had to depend on public transportation. Finally she realized that her lack of familiarity with the town was going to keep her from finding a place to live at a price she could pay. It was one more thing to turn over to Vince.

Anyway, it would be better to get the job first and then look for an apartment within walking distance. There was Erika's work to consider as well. She didn't know where the high school was located. She vacated the booth in favor of a big fat man with a cigar and a sample case, and made her way to Vince's store. Right now, she admitted, it was the only home she had.

Today he had a gift copy of Robert Browning's poems in the center of the window, an Edwardian offering in white, watered silk with a garland of roses on the front cover, and a frayed purple ribbon hanging out of the gilt-edged pages. She was glad that someone else had liked these fond and foolish volumes; she hoped the right person would come along to buy this one. The rest of the display—fans and a millefleur paperweight—she barely glanced at. The chimes tinkled twice as she opened the door and shut it again behind her.

Vince said, "Doll, am I glad to see you! Where have you been since breakfast time?"

"Organizing my entire life. Vince, where's a good hotel for a few days? Not too cheap or too expensive?"

"Single or double?"

"Why, I don't know." At least she didn't have to beat around the bush with Vince. He knew what the score was; he was on her side. At least, he was on Erika's side. It came to the same thing in the long run. She said, "That depends on her. I'll start looking for an apartment just as soon as—"

"Frances."

"What's the matter?"

"You're going to hate me," Vince said. He did look anxious. "Erika came down here, oh, around half-past ten, to see if I'd heard from you. I got the idea she expected you and you didn't show. You stayed at her place last night, was that what happened?"

"Till six this morning." Her mouth was dry. "Then I had to go home. I told her I'd be back. She should have waited. I was going up there as soon as I had it out with Bill."

"She acted like she was hurt because you left." Vince picked up a volume of essays from the counter and flipped through the pages, trying to look interested. "Or maybe puzzled. You must not have told her what you had to cope with at the other end of the line."

He put the book down and gave Frances a look of mixed

bravado and apology. "I spilled it. I'm sorry."

"What?" But she knew.

"That you had to account for your comings and goings to a husband."

"Oh God."

"Oh God is right. You must have forgotten to mention that you had any such thing."

"I didn't mean to hide it from her. You have to believe that." She laid a hand on his unresponding arm. "I didn't even think about it at first, it didn't seem to matter, and then I couldn't find any good way to bring it up. I was going to tell her the whole thing as soon as I broke away from him. Honestly."

Vince shrugged. "I take it you finally broke away. Or did you run into a cement mixer on the way down here?"

"Don't be like that."

"I believe you, all right. But will she?"

"What did she say?" She waited anxiously.

"Nothing. Not a mumblin' word. She simply walked out."

There was no handy answer for that. She stood looking at him, while the new world she had been building went up in a mushroom-shaped cloud. Job, apartment, and all.

He said nervously, "It's not good."

"Look, I left my husband this morning. For keeps. Told him I was going and walked out, like whatshername, that Ibsen girl. I told him why, too." She smiled. It hurt her swollen jaw. "All my clothes and stuff are at the Greyhound station in a locker, two big heavy suitcases. Would it be a bright idea if I just took the next bus out?"

"Where to?"

"Anyplace. I don't care."

"You want to kill her completely?"

"I don't want to hurt her at all, I'd sooner be thrown to the lions, but it looks like I can't help it. We were both happy last night," Frances said miserably. "I know she was happy. That makes it even worse."

"That was the impression I got, too. Only the people you care about can hurt you like she was hurt."

All her sureness had vanished away. She stood in the middle of the floor looking at him. "I don't know what to do," she said in a surprised voice. "What should I do?"

"Get an explanation to her some way. Look." His face was friendly now; he put his hand over her cold fingers, detaching them gently from his sleeve. "I had a fight with somebody I loved a lot, once. He hurt me, and I said so. I never want to see you again, I said. So he went away." Vince smiled. "I sat around for three months waiting for him to come back. I would have cut my tongue out and mailed it to him, special delivery, if it would have done any good."

Didn't he ever write, or anything?"

"Nope."

"That's terrible."

"Sure, he should have knocked me down and made me listen. Nobody meant anything, it was just a fight like people have. Only we kept getting in deeper."

"So what do I do?"

"It might not work, but what I'd do, I'd go and see her. Make her talk to you. She's a stubborn little bitch, and a good thing, she's had to be, but when she sees you the battle is half over."

"Maybe not."

But she knew she would go.

Vince said, "What have you got to lose? You want me to come with you?"

"No thanks. This is my problem. I got myself into it, I can get myself out of it."

"Let me know how you come out. I love both you kids."

"Sure."

She took a taxi. Any other way would take too long. The taxi went too slowly, as it was.

The door of Erika's house stood ajar to the hot summer air. Someone had hung a washing in the side yard. She went up, noting as she had the night before that the railing was really about to break through and fall. It was no place for Erika. She felt her shirt pocket to make sure her money was still there.

She knocked on Erika's door. There was no answer. She

called out, a silly thing to do, for if Erika were really angry she would be more likely to open to a knock—the landlady or a delivery boy—than to a voice she hated. Still no answer. Frances waited, hearing her own breathing, hoping to catch some little sound that would indicate the room was occupied. There was nothing. The place felt empty.

Either Erika wasn't there, or she was asleep, or else—Frances shut her mind quickly against any grimmer possibility. She went back down the rickety stairs onto the porch and sat on the top step in the shade. Should have brought a good book, she thought. Or some knitting. It may be quite a wait.

Even, maybe, forever.

She wouldn't do a thing like that. Would she? If she got desperate enough? It happened all the time. People jumping out of windows, taking an overdose of sleeping pills, cutting their throats.

Two little girls came out of the house next door, solemnly marked the front walk into squares with a piece of chalk and began to play hopscotch. They looked curiously at her. She tried to smile, but it made her face hurt. The bruise on her jaw was getting stiff.

A thin woman in purple slacks and a lace blouse, her hair in curlers, came up the walk with a sack of groceries. Frances looked at her, but she looked the other way. She went into the house. Frances could hear the clatter of her bargain-basement wedgies on the stairs.

It was very hot. Flies buzzed around her sweaty face. She brushed them away.

After what seemed like several hours—but the two little girls were still playing on the hopscotch walk, bickering shrilly—she went into the house again and climbed the stairs. The door was still locked and there was no sound. Maybe she's—maybe something has happened to her, she thought in terror. That's what Vince was thinking about. That's why he offered to come along.

The landlady would have duplicate keys. She walked slowly downstairs again, concocting a story. She had left her purse in

Miss Frohmann's room, and now Miss Frohmann seemed to be out. She found the door from which the curlered head had been thrust that first night, and rapped. There was no answer.

A thin young man coming down the stairs said pleasantly, "She works on Saturdays. Can I do anything for you?"

"You don't know when Erika Frohmann will be in, do you? I left something in her room." And that's no lie, she thought grimly.

"I didn't even know she was out. I guess that's not much help."

"Thanks anyway."

When he was gone, she took up her position again on the porch.

She ran through the history of her entire life, which from this vantage point seemed to be made up completely of failures and stupid mistakes. It was unbelievable that one person could do so many wrong things in such a short time, without help from anybody. I've never accomplished a thing, she thought miserably. I don't matter to one single person. I was going to be so much and lead such a wonderful life, and I can't even love one person without having it backfire.

She had been there half and hour or so when a light step on the walk made her look up. It was Erika, looking the way she always looked, wearing an old pair of pedal pushers and a T-shirt, with both arms around a big paper sack of groceries. At the sight of Frances she stopped short. Her face hardened.

Frances got slowly to her feet and stood foolishly at the top of the stairs, waiting.

Erika said, "Let me by."

"I have to see you."

"I know all about you." There was no anger in Erika's voice, only acceptance. She had expected something like this to happen. Anything else was too good to be true. "You're one of those two-way people, think you can live on both sides of the fence. When you feel like slumming you pick up a girl. Any girl foolish enough to believe you, I think. Then you go back to your husband and your big house."

Erika pushed roughly past her and ran into the house and slammed the door.

Frances heard her steps going up the stairs fast and angry.

17

"YOU CAN'T BLAME HER," VINCE SAID REASONABLY. "She's had about all she can take." He unfolded a dress, put it on a hanger and looked around for a place to store it. "I make a good maid, don't I?"

"You make a good friend. Here, this is the closet door over here, I think."

It was getting dark. The sky beyond the window was a soft pale gray, tinged with the orange and red reflections of neon signs. Vince had turned on all the lights in the hotel room: the overhead fixture with its glass dome, the thin-stemmed twin lamps on the dressing table, and the bed-head reading lamp inside its frilled silk shade, like a chocolate nestled in its paper cup. "Lower middle class," he said, looking around, "but it's the best you'll find in this town for the money. How are you paying for it?"

"In cash, silly. Oh no, I see what you mean—by the day."

"That's good. You won't be out anything when you locate a place of your own. You can move right in."

"I'm going back to Chicago if I don't get things straightened out pretty soon." Her voice shook. She bent to line up a pair of shoes under the bed. "Why are we unpacking all this stuff?"

"Keeps it from getting wrinkled." He unrolled a somewhat messy-looking pair of striped pajamas. Her engagement ring rolled to the floor. "Hey, look what I found. Do I get to keep it?"

"That's my social security." She made a dive for the ring. He reached it first and stood examining it critically. "Ought to be worth three or four hundred in a jewelry store, not so much if you pawn it. This is all you have to live on?"

She patted her chest. "Hear me crackle."

"Give it here."

She handed him her roll out of ten and twenty-dollar bills. He counted it and put it neatly back together with the ring in the center. "Pin your pocket good and tight. It may not seem like much to you right now, but you'll be in a hell of a fix if you lose it."

"I'm in a hell of a fix now, and it'll take more than money to get me out of it."

"It's nice to eat regularly even when your heart is broken. How do you feel?"

"My head hurts."

"That's because you haven't had anything to eat. Come on, let's get the rest of this junk put away and I'll take you out to dinner. It wouldn't hurt you to put on a clean shirt, either. That one smells like a backed-up sink drain."

"You're so romantic." The smile she gave him was puny, but it was a try. "I'll put on a dress if you want me to."

"Don't bother. We have a little chore to tend to after we eat."

"Like what?"

Vince unfolded a blue satin slip, gave it an appraising look, and laid it in the open dresser drawer. "Nice embroidery. Handmade? We're going to drag that stubborn brat our of her lair and make her listen to reason. It may take both of us, one to do the talking and one to hold her down, but it's worth a try."

"All right, but it won't do any good."

"You got any better ideas?"

She hadn't. "All right, pick me out a clean blouse. One that isn't full of wrinkles, if that's not too much to ask."

"I must say you're not a very good packer. Next time call me first, I'll show you how."

"I was in a hurry."

And where was Bill by this time, she wondered as she retreated to the bathroom with the fresh blouse in her hand. She could still go back to him if everything else failed. If she wakened lonely and frightened in the small hours, would she be tempted to call him?

She hurried back into the bedroom, buttoning. "Do one more thing for me, Vince? Take a dime and go to the pay phone—there's one in the lobby, I saw it when we came in—and call Bill. I'll write the number down for you. It's not listed yet."

"What do you want me to tell him?"

"Tell him I'm leaving town. He'll hear from my lawyer in a day or two. I wouldn't bother, but I don't want him to get the cops out after me."

"Suppose he says come home, all is forgiven, there's a light in the window?"

"Tell him to go to hell." She ran a light lipstick over her mouth, leaning to the mirror, and combed her hair. "Tell him *merde*, but tell him politely."

"That's my good girl. It wouldn't kill you to use a little powder or whatever you use," Vince advised, leaving. He put his head back in the door. "Your face is shiny."

She sat down on a straight chair beside the window and tried to decide what came next. She could still see Erika's pale, sad little face, set in something worse than hate: cold rejection. If she lived to be a hundred, she felt she would never forget that last look before Erika walked away, slamming the door shut between them.

Hate was the next thing to love, Vince had assured her. Indifference is the opposite of love. Be thankful if she hates you, it's not so far to go as if you were strangers.

Cold comfort.

If there was any hope in the whole horrible situation, it was Vince's steadfast kindness. She supposed he was on her side in this chiefly because he thought she might be good for Erika— why, God only knew, since all she had done so far was rouse the girl's hopes and then shatter them. But he had spent the entire day with her, finding a place for her to stay, looking after all the practical details she felt too distrait to handle, putting up with her idiotic crying. If she had a friend in the world, it was Vince.

She was tired. She ached all over, her head most of all. She was almost willing to take a heavy sedative, go to bed and let the whole thing work itself out on another day. Except that the break-of-dawn awaking, when her first drugged sleep was over, would have been unendurable.

Vince came back, grinning. "He sounded kind of bad—like he didn't know whether to be mad or worried. I made my voice as basso profundo as I could. Maybe he'll think you've run off with a better man."

"You're a stinker. What did he say?"

"Said you can come home, but make your mind up pretty soon. Said he'll contest a divorce if you start one."

"He won't get anywhere with it. Cruelty is a good ground in this state."

"I'll be your character witness. Or find a couple of straight-type girls, that always looks good in court. Seeing he hit you, that's really all you need, specially if you're not asking for support."

Frances shook her head. "Poor Bill. I must have been hell to live with. I'd like for him to be happy, and everything. Only let him not bother me."

"You'll be all right."

"I hope so. Did I hear you say something about dinner?"

"If you can think about food, your heart isn't broken."

He took her to a small dim restaurant tucked away between two large stores. She sat in a linen-covered table, with real candles throwing uneven shadows on everything, and blinked gratefully at Vince. "The girls used to come here," he said. "Kate and Erika. It was a special place of theirs." He frowned at the menu. "I thought you'd like to know about her."

"Yes. Only it's no use, probably."

"You have to go along on the basis that everything's going to be all right," Vince said. "You know, Erika was about the lone-somest person in the world till Kate came along. I couldn't even get very close to her, and we were friends for years, as much as she was friends with anybody. She lived in a world of her own."

"What was Kate like?"

"Medium size, brown hair, looked about like anyone else. She was an alcoholic and a depressive. Couldn't hold a job more than a few days. Erika found her when she was at the bottom, and took care of her. I don't know what happened between them," Vince said delicately, "they never talked about personal things much, but they were together for a couple of years and Kate got herself straightened out all right. They were happy. All you had to do was see them together and you knew they were happy."

"Maybe I'd better not try. I'm not sure I can come up to something like that."

"Oh, nuts. Anything's better than being half alive."

"I'm not so sure."

"You need a drink. Bourbon?" He ordered it. She tried to protest. "Would you rather have vodka, or something? I don't like it myself, but it's a free country."

"I don't want anything."

"I'm not going to get you crocked, I'm just loosening you up a bit."

The drink tasted better than she expected. When her glass was empty Vince ordered a second round. Now things were beginning to look a little blurry. When she turned her head, the room swung around with her. She said, "I feel sort of funny," and clutched the edge of the table for stability. Vince nodded. "Okay, I'll order you some food now."

She ate it, whatever it was. It didn't seem to have any flavor, but she could still handle a fork, so she decided that she hadn't had too much to drink. "I'm getting to be a sissy," she told him owlishly. "That was only two, wasn't it?"

"About one and a half. I finished the second one for you."

"Oh. Just so it wasn't wasted."

She felt fine, but something had happened to her sense of time and direction. She didn't know whether she had come in just a little while ago or whether she and Vince had been sitting around in that dim light for hours. She finished her meal and groped around for her handbag, then remembered that all the money she owned in the world was pinned inside her shirt pocket. That was funny. She composed her face into an expression of extremely solemnity and got to the door all right and stood peering out while Vince paid the check. It was quite dark now. The street lights glowed through the nights, and the store signs were all on. "I'm all right," she told Vince when he slipped a hand under her elbow. "Just a little fuzzy, that's all."

"On two drinks? Don't fall apart on me, we've got a busy evening ahead of us."

"What doing?"

He waved at a cab. It stopped. "The best defense is a good offense," he instructed her, helping her in. "We go to see Erika. If she hears your story and then tosses us out, that doesn't leave you much choice—but it's the best we can do."

"We can't get in."

"Sure we can. Remember?" He took an old-fashioned door key from his jacket pocket. "I've never used it before, but I keep forgetting to give it back. Pays to be a slob."

"She felt safe, knowing you could get in."

"Women dramatize everything so."

"Yeah. We're almost as bad as fairies."

"The street lights showed Erika's block shabby without romance. Vince paid the driver and stood with an arm around Frances's shoulder as he drove away. "Pray she isn't watching us out of the window," he said as they started up the porch steps.

Frances's heart was pounding so, she was afraid it would knock a hole in her chest. She said, "I can't."

"You have to. Come on."

She followed him. I'm getting pretty damn tired of these old stairs, she thought. He knocked lightly on Erika's unrevealing door. From the other side a muffled voice, startled, "Who is it? What do you want?"

"Me. Vince."

"I don't want to talk to anybody. I'm in bed. Please go away. I'll see you tomorrow."

"I have to see you."

"Vincent, I don't feel well. Please go away."

Frances looked at him. He unlocked the door and pushed it open. She stood against the rubbed wallpaper of the hall, shaking, afraid she was going to faint.

Vince said crossly, "Come in and shut the door. Do you want all the neighbors in here?"

She shook her head. He reached out a strong thin arm and

pulled her into the room, slamming the door shut behind her. At the sight of her, Erika grew very pale. She got up and stood facing them. "Please go away, or I'll scream. You can't break into somebody's home like this."

"Home," Vince said with a scornful glance around. "Sit down, Frances. The bed's all right."

Erika opened her mouth. Frances had no doubt she would yell if she felt like it. Vince reached out, lightning fast, and gave her a good slap that closed it. The sound was terrible. Frances cowered as though she were the one struck, putting a hand up to shield her face. Erika put a hand across her mouth and stood staring at him as though she couldn't believe her own senses.

"Damn right," Vince said as though she had asked a question. "Now you kids are even. Francie's husband popped her one this morning when she told him she was getting out. The silly bitch has been trying to get up enough nerve to leave for years, and she finally made it. You know why? Because she thought you wanted her. She thought you loved her, that's why. She couldn't end a bad marriage for her own sake, but she did it for you."

Frances said, "Vince, let me—"

"And what did you do? You should have been woman enough to trust her. But no, you have to act like a spoiled brat. You've been around a long time, you're no kid, you know who you can trust and who you can't trust," Vince said with a lovely disregard for logic. "Why are you sitting around sulking? Francie's been caught for years. Now she's finally made it—on your account. And what happens? You let her down."

Erika's lips quivered. "Nobody's going to sleep with me and some man too. I've met these people before. They're really straight. They come across the fence and play around and then they go back to their nice safe, straight life. I don't want any part of it."

Frances cleared her throat. "That's not so." Her voice sounded loud and strange in her own ears. "I tried. You don't end a marriage easily, not even a bad one. But I've hated every day of it."

"You'll only go back to your husband. It's better that way." But Erika was softening. Her voice was doubtful, and she looked at Vince to be reassured.

Frances shook her head. "I'll go away if you really want me to. I won't bother you anymore. Maybe I'll even find somebody else to love. But it won't be a man. I'm a lesbian, I'll never try to make it with a man again, but I can live alone if I have to." She knew, with a wonderful sense of freedom, that she was telling the truth at last. "Or maybe somebody will come along who's lonesome and likes me. But what I won't do, I won't be guilty of this terrible self-pity the way you have been."

She turned away. Erika looked at Vince. "Is that what you think? I've been faking."

"No," he said gently. "Not faking—just all wrapped up in yourself. That's all right for a while, but it's time now to grow up."

"I'm afraid."

"Sure you are. So'm I. So's everybody."

Erika said, "Yes." She looked around as though a door might open in the wall and let her out.

Frances said, "Erika."

Erika's face broke up. She said, "I don't know what to do next."

"Let me introduce you. Mrs. Ollenfield, this is my dear old friend, Miss Frohmann. I do hope you girls will like each other—you have so much in common. Like you're both queer as a pair of three-dollar bills."

Erika asked faintly, "Is my face bruised?"

Frances said indignantly, "I'll kill him if he ever hits you again." She glared at Vince, putting her arms protectively around Erika's thin shoulders.

Erika said, "Look." And burst into tears. At the sight of her face all puckered up Frances started crying too. There was nothing restrained about it.

Vince said, "Leave me out of here before I drown." He dropped his key on the bed. "Give me a call tomorrow, if you have the strength to."

Nobody paid him any attention.

When she heard the door close, Erika disentangled herself from Frances's arms and said, "I feel like a fool. I never cry."

"I never do either," Frances said in a shaky voice. "But when I do they can hear me ten miles away."

"What killed me," Erika said, refusing to be amused, "was thinking you were using me for an amusement. I should have known better."

"It was my fault for being such a coward. I should have left Bill years and years ago, when I found out about myself. Bake kept telling me. First I didn't think I could leave my son, but really I was only afraid."

"I didn't even know you had a son."

"He's a freshman in college. Married. They're going to have a baby." Frances looked stricken. "I'll be a grandmother. Can you care for a grandmother?"

"You are the youngest looking grandmother I know."

"Look," Frances said, "with Bake it was like being hit by lightning. You don't mind if I mention this just once, do you? It was the great big love of a lifetime. Then things went wrong, she drank too much, her friends were more sophisticated than I was, I wasn't brave enough to leave Bill—it was probably mostly my fault. Everything happened at once." She laid her hand on Erika's. "This time I'm not expecting it to be perfect. I'll fail you, we'll probably fight sometimes, but maybe we can talk things over and make a few compromises."

"There will be times when I don't want to talk to anybody, not even you."

"Then you can go into the bathroom and lock the door."

"Also I can't help thinking about Kate sometimes. You don't get over these things in one day."

"That's all right. I'll lie on the other side of the bed and think about all the wonderful girls I've made love to."

"I'm sure there were dozens." Erika's eyes crinkled into the unwilling beginning of a smile. "We're both getting older. Maybe we can make a more mature relationship, not so exciting, but a better one." She closed her thin fingers around Frances's wrist. "What you mean to me I can't begin to tell you. Only I tell you one thing, I don't want just an affair. I want a marriage."

"So do I. A trial one if you're not 100 percent sure, six months or a year so you won't feel trapped."

Erika shook her head. "You can leave any time you get tired of me. But please, no short-term contracts."

"All right." She laughed. "We'll have bills to pay and dishes to wash. I hate washing dishes."

"You can't scare me that way. I want you very badly."

Frances sighed. "I don't think I can live through another day like this."

"Let's not think about the dishes tonight. We didn't even buy them yet. Are you tired? Do you want to go to bed?"

"Not yet. I want a newspaper. I don't suppose there's a paper stand open within ten miles of here, this hour of the night."

"Sure, at the corner. Do you want to go by yourself, or can I walk along?"

"Come on. It's beautiful outside."

"Oh," Erika said joyfully, "do you like the night too?"

Stepping into the deep lake of shadow under overarching branches, they came into each other's arms. Frances said, "Hold me," and they stayed together until a car came along, its headlights picking them out. Frances broke away first. "That was a good sample. Do you want to walk all the way to the corner, or should we go back in?"

"No, first we buy you a paper."

The newsstand was next door to the little diner where she had eaten breakfast that morning, so long ago. Erika said, "I wish I had brought my pocketbook, I'd like a cup of coffee."

"I'm loaded. Listen."

Erika was shocked. "No! Why do you carry so much money in your shirt pocket?"

"It's my hope chest."

"About the hope I don't know, but it's a beautiful chest."

They found stools at the counter. The counterman said, looking at Frances's discolored eye and swollen chin with a great deal of interest, "Wasn't you in here this morning?"

"Sure, I'm back for my second cup."

He set the steaming cups down in front of them.

Frances unfolded the paper, turned to the Help Wanted page and refolded it. Her hands shook a little. "Got a pencil?"

The counterman said, "Here, take this, I'm not using it."

She began making check marks against the first column.

He said, "You girls mind keeping an eye on the register for a minute? I want to get my dishtowels out on the line."

"Sure, go ahead."

Erika put her hand down on the paper, blotting out Frances's view. "I don't mean to be curious," she said sweetly, "I know even married couples are entitled to a little privacy, but what are you doing?"

"Jobs. I'm going to get up early tomorrow—around noon, maybe—and go out and apply for a job. Or were you figuring to live on love?"

"Well," Erika said, "the landlady won't approve." She leaned her whole weight against Frances, a promise for the night that lay ahead. "It's a good beginning, though."

The Feminist Press is an independent, nonprofit literary publisher that promotes freedom of expression and social justice. Founded in 1970, we began as a crucial publishing component of second wave feminism, reprinting feminist classics by writers such as Zora Neale Hurston and Charlotte Perkins Gilman, and providing much-needed texts for the developing field of women's studies with books by Barbara Ehrenreich and Grace Paley. We publish feminist literature from around the world, by best-selling authors such as Shahrnush Parsipur, Ruth Kluger, and Ama Ata Aidoo; and North American writers of diverse race and class experience, such as Paule Marshall and Rahna Reiko Rizzuto. We have become the vanguard for books on contemporary feminist issues of equality and gender identity, with authors as various as Anita Hill, Justin Vivian Bond, and Ann Jones. We seek out innovative, often surprising books that tell a different story.

See our complete list of books at **feministpress.org**, and join the Friends of FP to receive all our books at a great discount.

THE FEMINIST PRESS
AT THE CITY UNIVERSITY OF NEW YORK
FEMINISTPRESS.ORG